Death By Malice
A Josiah Reynolds Mystery

Abigail Keam

Worker Bee Press

Death By Malice

ISBN 978 0 9979729 0 0

2 7 2017

Published in the USA by

Worker Bee Press
P.O. Box 485
Nicholasville, KY 40340

Abigail Keam

Acknowledgements

Thanks to my editor, Faith Freewoman

Artwork by Cricket Press
www.cricket-press.com

Book jacket by Peter Keam
Author's photograph by Peter Keam

3

By The Same Author

Death By A HoneyBee I
Death By Drowning II
Death By Bridle III
Death By Bourbon IV
Death By Lotto V
Death By Chocolate VI
Death By Haunting VII
Death By Derby VIII
Death By Design IX

The Princess Maura Fantasy Series

Wall Of Doom I
Wall Of Peril II
Wall Of Glory III
Wall Of Conquest IV
Wall Of Victory V

Last Chance For Love Series

Last Chance Motel I
Gasping For Air II
The Siren's Call III
Hard Landing IV
The Mermaid's Carol V

To my three dogs–a Mastiff, a Labrador, and a Peekapoo–devoted companions and friends. I'll meet you on the other side.

Prologue

Sandy Sloan knocked on my door. She waited several minutes before waving at the security camera. She knew it took me a long time to walk to the front door and check the security monitors. I had a bad leg that acted up from time to time and slowed me down.

Finally, I opened the door. "Hello, Sandy. What's cookin'?" I asked, looking down curiously at Sandy's mutt, Georgie.

"Josiah, I have a favor to ask. My mother has taken ill, and my husband is working very long hours. Can you take care of Georgie for a few days? Please. I'm in a real bind here."

I gave Sandy a long stare before I said yes, as Sandy's mother had died several years before. I know this for a fact since I had attended her funeral. What would cause Sandy to tell such a lie?

Wondering if I should call Toby, her husband, I asked, "Sure. I'll help, Sandy. Where ya going again?"

"That's great you'll take in Georgie," answered

Sandy, ignoring my question. She handed me Georgie's leash with the dog attached to the other end and a bag. "Here's all her stuff–her bed, toys, and food bowl. Can you spot me some of Baby's food until I get back?" I started to say something.

"Great. Thanks a lot," interrupted Sandy, kissing Georgie goodbye before hopping into her van.

Georgie and I watched forlornly while the disappearing vehicle rushed down the driveway, spraying gravel onto newly-mowed grass.

Georgie started to whimper.

I picked her up clumsily because Georgie was heavier than she looked. "Don't worry, Georgie. I'll take good care of you until Sandy comes back. You'll have fun while she's gone. You'll see."

Little did Georgie and I know that Sandy Sloan would soon become a missing person.

1

Sandy Sloan waited patiently in line until it was her turn for the bank teller. "I would like to close my account, please," she stated softly.

"Yes, Mrs. Sloan," replied the bank teller, pulling up her account on the computer screen. "You said you wanted to close your joint account?"

"Yes."

"Would you like that amount in the form of a cashier's check or shall we transfer it to another bank?"

"Cash please."

The bank teller tore his eyes from the computer to Mrs. Sloan's blotchy face. It was evident she had been crying. "Are you sure, Mrs. Sloan? That's a lot of cash to be carrying around."

"I'm sure. I want my money and I want it in cash. Please."

"Just one moment." The bank teller left his post and hurried over to the bank manager. He leaned down and whispered to the manager, who swiveled his head and looked in alarm at Mrs. Sloan.

Mrs. Sloan stared back.

Since the bank manager and Mrs. Sloan worshipped at the same church, he thought he could be a little more familiar than usual. He walked over. "Sandy, Tom tells me you want to close your account for cash. Is that right?"

"Yes. Is there problem?"

"Not really, but we don't advise people to carry such large amounts from the bank. They could be robbed."

"Do you have the money in the bank or not?"

"Yes. We can cover it."

"Then I want my money now. In cash."

The bank manager went to the front door and looked out into the parking lot. There were no other cars, but Sandy's. He quickly left the bank and went over to her navy minivan, checking the inside. No one was in it. Scratching his head, the bank manager wondered if someone was forcing her to take the money out like he had seen on TV crime programs. He went back inside and questioned Sandy. "Is something wrong, Sandy? Is someone forcing you to cash in your account?"

"No. I just want my money. Is there a law against closing out my account and getting my money in cash?"

"No, ma'am."

"I want my money. Now. Today."

Knowing he had no choice, the bank manager nodded to Tom. "Give Mrs. Sloan what she wants." He tugged at his shirt collar. "I hope you know what you're doing. You could tell me if something is wrong."

Sandy flashed the bank manager a brilliant smile. "Nothing is wrong, but thanks for looking out for me. I won't forget it. Really, I won't."

The bank manager left Sandy standing at Tom's station while the teller closed out the account. He just couldn't shake the feeling that something about this was not right. Not right at all.

2

Sandy scattered bills throughout the living room. The total she had taken from the bank was thirty-two thousand dollars.

Content, Sandy surveyed the money thrown helter-skelter on the furniture and the hardwood floor. Locking the front door, she strained to pick up the five-gallon gas can she had brought in from the barn. Carefully, she poured the gasoline around the room all the way to the kitchen. *There's no turning back now*, she thought to herself. Standing inside the kitchen, Sandy struck a match and threw it into the living room.

It died.

She struck another one and threw it.

It died too.

Determined, she struck one more match and placed it in the large kitchen matchbox. After a few seconds, the box became alive with fire. Smiling, Sandy threw it into the living room.

FLASH!

Tall flames danced about the living room floor and the furniture. Soon the entire room became engulfed in fire.

Sandy emitted a maniacal laugh, dancing around in the kitchen doorframe, watching the money and the living room burn.

She even laughed when the fire licked her toes.

3

It had been several hours since Sandy had left. Holding Georgie, I went into the great room where Walter Neff had taken up residence on my mid-century blue-green couch, with his unshaven face, stained T-shirt, and much-too-snug tighty-whities.

"Walter, for the last time, would you please put on a pair of britches? When I said you could stay with me while you recuperated, it did not mean I was willing to see your junk on a daily basis."

"I'd be glad to put on my pants if I had some help," he whined, trying to look pathetic.

"You can put on your own pants. In fact, your physical therapist said you're well enough to live on your own now."

Walter shook his head. "No Toots, you musta' heard wrong. She said I would be well enough SOON."

I was determined to stay firm with this rascal. "NO! She said you were well enough NOW!"

Almost in tears, I sat down hugging Georgie. "Walter, you've been here for six weeks–six very long weeks. I gotta tell ya–you're driving me nuts. I don't mean to be personal, but you never wear clothes, you talk with your mouth full while eating, and you stay in the bathroom for hours doing God knows what. I need my privacy. I need quiet. I need to pass the guest bathroom without having to put on a gas mask. In short–I NEED YOU TO GO HOME!

"Walter, I'm begging you. Haven't I been good to you? I acquired a large sum of money for that ruby Liam left, and put it in your bank account. I could have kept the money and never told you about the ruby, but I did the right thing by you. I let you recuperate at the Butterfly after you were released from the hospital. Wouldn't you say I've been a good buddy to you? So now, I'm asking for a favor in return. GET THE HELL OUT OF MY HOUSE! Please, Walter, please. I can't take much more."

I buried my face in Georgie's fur. She was now squirming, trying to get out of my grip and hide somewhere. Obviously, Georgie was a lover, not a fighter.

Walter opened his mouth to say something, but was cut short when Eunice banged open the front door and hurried over to the phone in the great room.

"Eunice, what is it?"

"My cell phone is dead. I have to use the landline."

She waved at Walter and me, motioning us to be quiet while she dialed. "Hello? Hello? I want to report a fire." Eunice rapidly gave the address. "Hurry please. A house is going up in flames. Hurry!" Eunice slammed down the phone. "I have to sit down. My nerves are frayed."

I pulled a rocking chair over for Eunice since Walter hadn't moved his flabby carcass, although he did cover himself with an afghan my mother had crocheted. *Made a mental note to get the afghan fumigated.*

Rushing into the kitchen, I got a glass of cold water for Eunice. After handing her the glass, I asked, "Would you like a little bourbon?"

"This will do nicely, thank you. I just have to catch my breath." Eunice squinted at Georgie squirming in my arms. "Isn't that Sandy Sloan's dog? What's she doing here?"

"Sandy brought her over earlier. She said the strangest thing."

Eunice interrupted, "Sandy brings her dog over this morning and now her house is on fire? That sounds odd. Did she say she was going back to her house?"

"She said she was going to her mother's, but her mother is dead," I replied, worried that Sandy had done something awful. "I hope she's okay. Should we go to the house to help?"

Eunice tilted her head to listen. "I hear the fire trucks coming. I think we should stay here, Jo. We'd just be in the way. If there's bad news, we'll know soon enough."

She took another sip of water before commenting, "Why are you clutching Sandy's dog so tightly?"

"Baby keeps holding Georgie down with one of his paws and engulfing the little dog's head in his mouth. I'm simply trying to keep Georgie safe before she ends up down Baby's throat. I locked Baby up, but he keeps getting out, so I'm holding Georgie out of danger. Ah, speak of the devil."

Baby, my two-hundred-pound Mastiff, trotted into the room, sniffing the air. He caught Georgie's scent and made straight for me. I held Georgie high when Baby lunged at me. "Stop, Baby! You're being a pest–like Walter."

Walter sneered, "Oh, that's a funny one, Toots."

Eunice ordered, "BABY! STOP! Lie down and behave."

Eunice was the only person Baby feared and promptly obeyed. He sneezed to show his displeasure, but lumbered over to his dog bed in the corner of the room and plopped down, glaring at me like it was my fault.

Eunice also directed her ire at me. "Put that dog down. Baby's not going to bother her anymore–are you, Baby?" Eunice turned, giving Baby the evil eye.

Baby shifted so he didn't have to see her, but he didn't race over to eat Georgie when I put her down.

"Whose house is on fire?" questioned Walter, happy that the conversation had drifted from the subject of him leaving the Butterfly.

"Sandy and Toby Sloan. They're two farms down from the Butterfly," said Eunice.

"I hope Sandy and Toby are safe," I remarked, glancing at Georgie who was now attempting to get her mouth around one of Baby's dinosaur-sized bones. My mind raced through hundreds of scenarios that might explain Sandy's odd behavior today.

Was it a coincidence that Sandy dropped Georgie off the very morning her house was ablaze?

Was the fire an accident or had something more sinister occurred?

And where, oh where, was Sandy Sloan at this moment?

4

Two days later, Eunice, Belle, Georgie, and I
trod along the path leading along the Palisades. While my
neighbors on my left, which included Lady Elsmere, had
direct access to the river, I and my neighbors on my right
lived on the beautiful cliffs overlooking the Kentucky
River. We either used Lady Elsmere's road to the river,
or we went to the John Craig Ferry landing to gain access
to the water.

But we were not interested in the river. We were
interested in Sandy's house. There had been nothing
about the fire on TV or in the paper, and we hadn't heard
from either Toby or Sandy. We were worried, tense, and
just plain concerned about our friends, so we decided to
have a look-see for ourselves.

Our walk took about ten minutes, and when we finally
arrived–my, oh my–what we saw.

"This is much worse than I anticipated," declared
Eunice, looking at the still-smoldering debris.

It was indeed a terrible sight for most of the front of the house had been burned to the ground.

I shook my head in bewilderment. "Why has nothing been in the paper about this? And why hasn't Sandy come for Georgie?"

Speaking of Georgie, she strained at her leash until she yanked it out of my hand. Rushing over to the charred debris, she began pawing through it.

"Hey, get that dog out of here! This is an investigation site."

Startled, Eunice and I both swung around. Baby growled as I pulled out my taser.

A man about my age, dressed in a thick white jumpsuit complete with booties, gloves, and a hoodie, came around a large burnt beam lying upright against the still-standing fireplace. He picked up a whimpering Georgie, and ducked under the crime scene tape. "Don't you see this tape? It says for you to stay out," he barked, handing Georgie to me.

Baby growled again as he began thumping his tail against my bad leg, which felt like someone whipping me with a tree branch. I could tell Baby was getting very agitated.

"Excuse me, but I wouldn't move suddenly. This dog is a trained attack animal, and if I give the word, he'll tear you apart."

"Hogwash," refuted the man, reaching down and petting Baby. "He's doing what comes naturally to an English Mastiff."

At this point, Georgie squirmed so hard I almost dropped her.

"Here, here. Hold her like this. She'll feel more secure in your arms."

"The problem is I don't want to hold her. She's heavy for a little dog."

"I'm sorry, but I'm in the middle of an examination of this site, and you two with your dogs can't be here. It's as simple as that."

Eunice spoke up. "We are friends of Toby and Sandy Sloan. In fact, this is Sandy's dog." She pointed to the little mutt.

"Really?" said the man, looking at us with new interest.

Eunice continued, "Sandy left her dog with us on the day the house burned, but she hasn't been back for her. Have you heard from Sandy or Toby Sloan?"

"What are both your names?"

"You first, buddy. How do we know you're really an investigator? You could be a looter," I accused.

Nonplussed, the man replied, "My name is Hunter Wickliffe, and I'm investigating this fire."

"I'm Josiah Reynolds, and this is my business partner, Eunice Todd. We came over to see if Toby or Sandy might be here. Neither one is answering their phone."

I spotted a look of recognition on Hunter Wickliffe's face when I said my name, but it faded very quickly. "I should have known with the Mastiff," he muttered.

Confused, I gave him the once-over again. If I had met him before I didn't remember, but then I don't remember a lot these days. However, he did look oddly familiar. I just couldn't place him.

Eunice asked, "They're not dead, are they?"

"We haven't finished sifting through the debris, but neither one has shown up to see about their house."

"They were not in the fire," I stated.

Hunter Wickliffe asked, "Why do you say that?"

"Because their vehicles aren't here," I replied. "That means they weren't here for the fire." I didn't mention that either Toby or Sandy could have started the fire and then left, and I was favoring Sandy at the moment.

Hunter Wickliffe gave me an amused look of approval. "He said you were smart."

I asked, "Who said that about me? Have we met before?"

Hunter Wickliffe ignored my questions.

Eunice turned to me. "Is there anyone we can call who might tell us whether they're safe?"

I answered, "They never talked about their families much. Sandy did have a brother near Charleston somewhere, but I wouldn't know who to contact."

"It's whom."

"Excuse me?" I fired back, shooting Hunter Wickliffe an irritated glare.

"It's whom, not who," he answered with a pedantic air.

I felt like I was back in my Freshman English class, being berated by my teacher. "Listen, mister. I'm worried sick about my neighbors, and wondering what to do with their dog. This is not the time for you to correct my grammar. You can go ****"

"Jo, you forget yourself," admonished Eunice, elbowing me. "I'm very sorry my friend used those low-class words. She hasn't been herself for a while. She's usually more polite." Eunice thought for a second. "Well, sometimes Mrs. Reynolds is more polite." She began pulling me away. "C'mon, Josiah. Let's go."

"Wait a minute, ladies. I'll need to interview you both, since it seems you had contact with Mrs. Sloan on the day her house burned. You might have useful information."

I was clutching Georgie and pulling at Baby's collar, giving Mr. Wickliffe the silent treatment.

Eunice answered after taking the squirming Georgie from me. "You can find us at the Butterfly. The address is . . ."

"Don't bother. I know where Mrs. Reynolds resides."

"The code to the gate is . . ."

"I know the code."

Eunice and I exchanged glances.

"How do you know the code to my gate?" I blurted out.

Hunter Wickliffe answered, "A little bird told me."

"I demand to know."

"Mrs. Reynolds, I assure you that I work with law enforcement, and you have nothing to fear from me. I

22

will be in touch to arrange an interview with you both very soon. Please excuse me, but I need to finish examining the house. I'm on a schedule." Hunter Wickliffe turned and went back inside the smoldering house.

The fact that a stranger knew my address and the code to my fancy electronic gate was not good.

Not good at all.

5

It was a bright, cheerful afternoon four days later, when Hunter Wickliffe sat at the Nakashima table in my great room. He handed me his business card. "Please call me Hunter."

"You may call me Mrs. Reynolds." Studying the card, I said, "So you're a forensic psychiatrist." I looked at the other man sitting beside Hunter. "And who might you be?"

The gentleman handed me his card and showed a shield as well. "I am the Fire Department investigator for this case. My name is David Barbaro."

"I see." I gestured to the chair beside me. "This is my attorney, Shaneika Mary Todd."

Both men nodded in acknowledgement.

Hunter shook Shaneika's hand. "We met yesterday when we interviewed Ms. Todd's mother. I'm curious as to why you both feel you need a lawyer present to do a routine interview."

Shaneika and I chuckled.

I replied, "I don't talk to anybody above the rank of dogcatcher without a lawyer present. As for Mrs. Todd, I can't tell you why she wanted her daughter representing her, Mr. Wickliffe."

Hunter Wickliffe looked impatient as he took out a legal pad and a form from his expensive leather briefcase. "As I requested–call me Hunter. May we begin, please?"

I nodded.

"State your full name, please."

"Josiah Louise Reynolds."

"Age?"

"Fifty-two, soon to be fifty-three, and I'm white, as well," I replied, leaning over trying to get a look at the list of questions.

Hunter looked up and said, "I can see that, Mrs. Reynolds. There is no need to be defensive."

"Was I defensive? I thought I was being sarcastic."

"They're one and the same. We are just trying to do our jobs."

"Then tell me what happened to my friends."

"We were hoping you'd throw some light on the situation."

Mr. Barbaro interjected, "May we continue?" He looked at his watch.

"How well did you know the Sloans?" Hunter asked.

"Pretty well. I was closer to Sandy."

Hunter asked, "Why was that?"

I frowned. "Besides the obvious, Sandy was an artist, one of the best. I love art, so naturally Sandy and I were friends. I used to teach art history at UK."

"I see you enjoy paintings," commented Hunter, looking at the concrete back wall of the great room. "You have quite a collection."

"It used to be larger, but I had to sell some to keep the bill collectors from tar and feathering me."

Hunter waved a pencil at the paintings. "Any of those by Sandy Sloan?"

I turned and pointed. "The large landscape of the river on the right."

The men appraised the painting. David Barbaro made a brief sketch of it in his notes.

Hunter chewed on his pencil's eraser while studying the painting. "Did Sandy always paint landscapes?"

"Mrs. Sloan."

"What?"

"Call her Mrs. Sloan. Show some respect. She is not and was not your friend. You should not use her first name."

Hunter shot Shaneika a look of disbelief.

Shaneika leaned forward. "I think it would be best if everyone uses last names with the proper prefixes during the interview. Mrs. Reynolds believes strangers and children should not address adults by their first name without permission."

"Or their elders," muttered Hunter.

"What was that?" I asked.

"May we call you Josiah for convenience sake?" asked Hunter.

"No, you may not."

Hunter drew back in the chair. "Okay, then. Let's proceed. Did Sandy, err, Mrs. Sloan always paint landscapes?"

"Yes, she was a plein air painter."

Mr. Barbaro asked, "What's that?"

"It's French meaning open air. It describes painters who paint on-site rather than in a studio," I replied.

Hunter asked, "Did you think she was a good painter?"

I replied, "She has a national reputation. Sandy is very good. You keep using past tense. Should that tell me something?"

"Do you have any more of her paintings?"

"Just the one. She's out of my price range now."

"Did—does she ever work out of her house?"

"Yes, she had a back porch converted into a studio."

"Is that where she stores her paintings?"

"Yes, and they had better still be there, because I noticed the back porch had not burned."

Hunter Wickliffe and David Barbaro wrote furiously on their notepads.

Looking up from his writing, Hunter asked, "Can you tell us when you last saw Toby Sloan?"

"I haven't seen Toby for weeks. Maybe a month."

"Sandy Sloan?"

"It was six days ago, about nine in the morning."

Both men jotted down the information.

"What was she wearing?" asked Mr. Barbaro.

Shaneika interjected, "Gentlemen, I need to have only one person ask the questions. Mrs. Reynolds has had health issues since her accident several years ago, and double-teaming might throw her memory off. I'm sure you understand."

Both men nodded in agreement and looked at me with wary curiosity, as though I was a basket of bruised fruit.

Maybe I was. I took my time responding. "Um, she was wearing a red blouse over jeans and tennis shoes, I think."

"Were the jeans short or long pants?" Hunter asked.

"Long."

"What kind of blouse was Mrs. Sloan wearing? Did it have any buttons?"

"It was more like a T-shirt. Cotton. Yes, now I remember. The shirt was definitely a red cotton T-shirt. The kind you pull over your head."

Both men wrote furiously on their respective notepads.

Hunter looked up. "Can you describe her shoes?"

I shook my head. "I'm sorry. I really didn't notice. It could have been tennis shoes, or sandals for that matter. I just have a faint impression she was wearing tennis shoes, but I couldn't describe them to you. I couldn't swear to her shoes."

Hunter asked, "How would you describe Mrs. Sloan's demeanor?"

"She seemed chipper, but the conversation was odd."

"Can you be more specific?"

"Sandy asked me to watch her dog, Georgie, because she was going to help her mother, who was ill."

"And?"

"Well, that's the problem. Her mother's been dead for some time."

"Did you say anything to her about it?"

I shook my head before taking a sip of water from a glass on the table. "No. I just took Georgie."

"Why didn't you confront her?"

I sighed. "Sandy has had issues in the past. She sometimes gets confused. My first thought was she wasn't taking her medication. The last thing I wanted to do was confront a person having some sort of a mental episode when I was alone."

"Were you afraid of her?"

"Not really. I just didn't want to deal with a scene. I go out of my way to avoid confrontation."

Hunter Wickliffe looked up from his notes in disbelief. "Could have fooled me," he muttered.

"What was that?" I asked. "I can't hear you when you mumble."

Ignoring my remarks, Hunter pushed on. "Has Mrs. Sloan ever been violent?"

"Not with me, but with her husband, Toby."

"Can you tell me what you know about that?"

"Toby ran over here claiming Sandy came at him with a butcher knife."

"When was that?"

"About six months ago, I guess."

"What happened?"

"I called the police. They took Sandy in for an evaluation, and Toby went home."

"Did she attack the police?"

"I heard they found Sandy calmly eating a piece of pecan pie with a glass of milk. She even offered them some."

"Do you happen to know what the professional evaluation indicated?"

"I don't know. Neither Sandy nor Toby ever discussed the incident with me again."

"Did you believe Toby's story?"

"I know Sandy to be a sweet and gentle person. She does have a bipolar disorder and suffers from depression, but I've never known her to be violent."

"You didn't answer my question. Did you believe Mr. Sloan's story?"

I hesitated before speaking. "Well, no. I like Toby very much, but I can't imagine Sandy chasing him around the living room with a butcher knife. Toby likes to exaggerate."

"Would there be any reason Mrs. Sloan would be angry with her husband?"

I shot Shaneika a quick look.

"Mrs. Reynolds, we need to know all the facts if we are to help your friends."

"Word drifted around that Toby was messing with some filly over in Winchester, and wasn't being very discreet about it."

"Do you know the woman's name?"

"I learned about it from my neighbor, Lady Elsmere."

Hunter Wickliffe sighed. "Please answer the question."

"Carol Elliott."

"Did Lady Elsmere tell you how she knew?"

I noticed he didn't ask who Lady Elsmere was. Everyone either knew Lady Elsmere or had heard of her. I answered, "She never divulges her sources, but she knows everything going on around here. Lady Elsmere is an absolute whore for gossip."

"Another woman sounds like a perfect excuse for a wife to become angry and chase her husband with a butcher knife."

"I'm not sure Sandy knew. She never mentioned it to me."

"Could Mrs. Sloan have started the rumor for some unknown purpose?"

"No. Sandy is a shy person. This is something she would not want known about her personal life."

"Do you believe the rumor about Mr. Sloan having an affair?"

"I don't have an opinion, but where there's smoke, there's fire." I winced at my choice of words. "Like I said, I like Toby. He can be very charming, but he is a sneaky son-of-a-gun."

"About what?"

"Oh, silly things, nothing serious."

"Give me an example."

"I gave an outdoor party once. Sandy and Toby came early to help. I had a large tub of ice filled with beer outside on the terrace. When I checked the tub before the party started, most of the beer was gone. I asked Toby about the missing beer. He told me he saw the Dupuy boys take the beer."

Hunter Wickliffe interrupted, "Excuse me. Who are the Dupuy boys?"

"They are the grandsons of Charles Dupuy, who is Lady Elsmere's heir."

Hunter raised an eyebrow while David Barbaro formed his mouth to make a silent whistle. They both knew that would involve millions.

I continued, "They were helping me also. Well, the boys were young teenagers at the time, so it was plausible, but I had a hunch. I checked the back of Toby's pickup and found the beer under some tarps."

"What happened?"

"I put the beer back and didn't say a word about it."

"How did Mr. Sloan respond?"

"Nothing. He didn't act guilty or offer an excuse or

an apology. Nothing. If I remember correctly, he had a good time, but he and Sandy left early."

"Why do you think Mr. Sloan chose to run to your house when he claimed he was being attacked? Why didn't he go to one of his closer neighbors or call on his own phone?"

"Maybe his phone was dead. The neighbors on the right were in Florida, and they don't have a landline, just cell phones. The neighbor between the Sloans and me is a mean old fart. If you were on fire, he wouldn't pee on you unless there was a buck in it for him. Sorry for the analogy, but there it is."

Why did I keep bringing up fire?

The corners of Hunter's mouth turned up, but quickly faded. "Do you know of any insurance policy the Sloans have on their property?"

"No."

"Have you had any contact with either Sandy or Toby Sloan since the fire?"

"I have not."

"Do you know of anyone who has had contact with Sandy or Toby Sloan?"

I shook my head. "I'm worried sick about them. If you're asking me about them, that means they're still alive, and you didn't find any bones in the fire debris." I leaned back in my chair. "Thank the Lord."

Hunter said, "I'm sure you understand we can't comment on anything, since the incident is still under investigation."

Shaneika agreed. "We understand, but any
information you might give Mrs. Reynolds will be
appreciated—after you finish your report, of course. Mrs.
Reynolds is taking care of Mrs. Sloan's dog and would
like to be relieved of this obligation."

Hunter asked, "What's the dog's name?"

I answered, "Georgie after Georgia O'Keeffe."

Mr. Barbaro butted in while making notations.
"Who's that?"

"A woman artist who painted large flowers that
symbolized female genitalia, but she always denied it, of
course," I said. "Not Sandy Sloan, but Georgia
O'Keeffe.

"Oh!" said David Barbaro, looking up from his notes,
rather embarrassed.

"Just one more question," queried Hunter, ignoring
my banter. "Do you know of any reason why Sandy or
Toby Sloan, either together or separately, would set fire
to their property?"

So the Fire Department was thinking along the same
lines as me. I was wondering when the question of arson
might come up. It had bothered me that Sandy had taken
such pains to make sure Georgie was safe and away from
the house on the day of the fire, but I still couldn't
believe it of either one of them.

I answered, "Both Sandy and Toby loved their house.
They poured hours and money into making it their
dream home."

The men put their notes in their respective briefcases
and stood.

David Barbaro shook my hand and nodded to Shaneika. "We'll be in touch if we have any more questions."

Hunter Wickliffe declared, "I'm sure we'll meet again, Mrs. Reynolds."

"Not if I can help it," I said. I had taken a dislike to the man, and as usual, didn't bother to hide it. Maybe he reminded me of Teddy McPherson, who had killed Bunny Witt and tried to kill me too. Hunter Wickliffe was handsome like Teddy, and slick, too. My defenses went up immediately the first time I laid eyes on him.

Shaneika saw the men to the front door and watched the security monitors until she saw their car turn onto Tates Creek Road. She came back into the great room. "That wasn't as brutal as I thought it was going to be."

"As long as they don't try to finger me for causing the fire," I answered. "You don't think Sandy or Toby could have set their own house on fire?"

"I didn't know them. Just met them briefly at Lady Elsmere's parties. I know people do set fire to their houses all the time for the insurance money."

"Were these the same questions they asked your mother?"

"More or less."

"What does that mean?"

"It means, more or less. Conducting interviews is standard procedure. They're doing their jobs, Josiah. They're not gunning for you. They are simply trying to find out what happened. Try to keep your natural paranoia in check. They're interested in you because Sandy brought her dog to you on the morning of the fire. It makes sense she would contact you to get her dog back."

"If she's alive, that is."

"That's the sixty-four-thousand-dollar question."

"What should I do?"

"Wait, and if Sandy shows up, call the police."

"And Georgie?"

"If she's a burden, take her to the pound in a couple of weeks if Sandy doesn't show."

"No. She might be, you know, snuffed out if she isn't adopted."

"Then keep her. She's little and cute. Doesn't take up much room."

"Baby doesn't get along with her. They're always fussing with each other."

"You spoil Baby too much. Let Mother handle the situation, or give the dog to someone."

I picked up Georgie, who had been contentedly gnawing on one of Walter's house slippers, and gave her a squeeze. "Don't worry, Georgie. I won't let any harm come to you. You can stay as long as you need." I scratched her behind the ears.

Georgie returned the affection with a wet tongue lick to my face.

"Isn't she the cutest little thing?"

Shaneika smirked. "I had a feeling you wouldn't give her away. You've already fallen in love."

"It's better for me to fall in love with a dog than a man. I don't seem to have good luck with men. Every man I've ever loved hit the road, but dogs have stuck with me through thick and thin. If I had to choose between a man and a dog—no contest. The dog stays."

Shaneika laughed as she grabbed her purse and briefcase. "I hope you and Georgie will be very happy together." She looked at her watch. "I have to go. I'm supposed to be in court in less than an hour. Now remember, if Sandy Sloan calls—contact the police."

"I will. I promise."

"Be good, Josiah. And if you can't be good, don't get caught."

Hmm. Shaneika had a sneaking suspicion I was gonna be bad.

So did I.

6

I didn't hear anything from Sandy or Toby, although I kept close to the house for several weeks. Nothing. Just an eerie silence. No phone calls. No letters. No telegrams. No one stopping by to say that they had seen them. No gossip about them from Lady Elsmere.

It was as though the world had swallowed them up.

The only thing in the paper about the fire was one paragraph stating the fire had occurred. No other details.

I decided to put the tragedy aside and get on with the business of living.

One item on my agenda was getting Walter Neff out of the Butterfly.

Even Eunice, who had the patience of Job, said he had to go. He was constantly pestering Eunice when she was planning a reception or wedding at the house.

Eunice had carved out an office in my library, and even stayed over when her workload was heavy. It saved her lots of traveling time to and from Versailles where she lived. But the time she saved in traveling was wasted due to Walter and his many demands. "He has to go, Josiah," she insisted.

"I'm working on it," I replied. Somehow, I needed to figure out a way to make Walter want to leave, but for the time being, I put those thoughts aside.

It was time to take a jaunt into the outside world.

Since I didn't schedule or plan the events at the Butterfly, I was free during the down times, which gave me a good excuse to get out of the house.

I had ordered papaw, mulberry, and apple trees, which I wanted to plant on the farm for the animals. I had received word they had come in at a nursery on Old Frankfort Pike.

I loaded Baby and Georgie into my Prius. Thank goodness both of them loved road trips. Georgie had settled in to living with us, and proved to be a loving companion. Baby grudgingly accepted her and, for the most part, left Georgie alone. However, when Georgie wanted to be loved on, Baby would thunder toward her, and butt the little dog out of the way with his massive head so he could be petted instead.

Methinks Baby is jealous.

Baby and I are still working on good manners, but really, who am I to scold Baby about manners?

It's not that I'm mean. I try to do the right thing. It's that I don't take the trouble to be nice anymore. I've gone through too much.

You know my story. Don't I have right to be angry?

My husband left me for a younger woman. My boyfriend ran out on me. I've lost most of my money. My dog was attacked and lost an eye. I was almost murdered on several occasions, hit over the head, and my friends were shot up.

My body is so busted, it will never be the same again. I walk with a limp, can't hear worth a nickel, and struggle with pain every day. And here's a lovely tidbit. My kidneys are threatening to shut down. So there you are.

All of which adds up to this: I don't give a tinker's damn if anyone thinks I'm bitter. I am!

People get nice and good mixed up. Some of the most wicked people in history have had polished manners, and were so charming their victims never saw their demise coming, whether that played out on a personal or national stage.

Enough of that tantrum.

It was a beautiful jaunt over RT 169 and Highway 33, driving through Versailles to Old Frankfort Pike, one of the most scenic roads in the Bluegrass. Baby, Georgie, and I were happily speeding along on Old Frankfort Pike when I spied Franklin's red Smart car ahead of us.

Curious, I slowed down.

What was Franklin doing on Old Frankfort Pike?

And in the middle of a workday?

Even though I considered Franklin a great friend, I knew little about him. He didn't discuss his people except to say they were a family of doctors, and were devastated when he choose not to become one. Sometimes he mentioned off-handedly his father was dead. Other times he said he was sharing the holidays with his old man, so who knows what's going on?

I do know Matt, my best friend, has never met anyone in Franklin's family. I thought it odd since Franklin was so proud of Matt and the new baby. You'd think he'd want to show them off.

My good angel whispered it was none of my business what Franklin might be up to, but my busybody angel shouted—*follow him*!

I chose the latter. What can I say in my defense? Nothing. I'm a curious old biddy, that's all.

Franklin turned abruptly into a driveway that had an ancient, stone, ivy-covered guardhouse safeguarding an ornate iron gate fifteen feet high, the kind of gate rich people install to keep the great unwashed out. You know—people like me.

The gate was hung from majestic limestone columns topped off with stone lions poised to pounce on intruders.

Traditional non-mortar limestone rock walls, typical in the Bluegrass, additionally protected the property. By the look of the construction of the stacked rocks, I could tell either the Irish or slaves, who were taught by the Irish, had built the walls before the Civil War.

The curved driveway was lined with oak trees and disappeared behind a stand of redbud trees. Usually, this kind of estate boasted an antebellum mansion containing very, very expensive antique furniture with a Jag or a Mercedes sitting out front.

Franklin entered a code into the keypad. The gates slowly swung open and his car sped down the drive.

Did Franklin have a well-heeled new boyfriend? Was our lad headed for an impromptu afternoon tryst?

Matt and Franklin's relationship had warmed up some since Matt's recovery from gunshot wounds, but it wasn't exactly hot. They were more like close friends, who had a lot of history between them, spending time together. So it wasn't out of the realm of possibility Franklin had found a new *love* interest.

I wouldn't have blamed him. Matt had treated Franklin abominably in the past, but Franklin, with his sweet nature, always forgave.

Still, I wanted to see what Franklin was up to. I pulled into the entrance before the imposing iron gates.

Hmm, the keypad might present a problem.

Excited, Georgie jumped, jumped, jumped, attempting to get into the driver's seat while Baby managed to wedge his head out my open window.

"Behave, you two," I complained. "I'm trying to think."

Baby and Georgie ignored me.

"Out of the way," I ordered, pushing Baby's head aside as he was obstructing the keypad.

Figuring I had nothing to lose, I randomly punched buttons.

BINGO!

The gate slowly squeaked open. Not trusting the gate, I rushed through the opening. It was neglected, as was most of the estate. The fields were not mowed. Leaves and debris were scattered across the driveway. I had to swerve several times to avoid large fallen branches.

An old tobacco barn on a distant rolling hill looked like it might fall down if a stiff wind blew its way.

It reminded me of my farm before Matt and Shaneika restored it while I was convalescing in Key West.

Someone was down on his luck.

The house appeared when I rounded a bend. Just as I had expected. It was a classic antebellum dwelling, two stories high, built of red brick with a portico extending the length of the house and anchored by white round Ionic columns.

There were four wide, floor-to-ceiling windows on the first floor, two on each side, which could be opened during the summer for cross ventilation. The front entrance was comprised of two doors, painted white, and probably made of solid oak.

The second floor boasted windows matching the first floor, with Juliet balconies adorned by ornate white iron railings.

If there hadn't been weeds sprouting everywhere, the house would have been stunning. As it was, it stood as a sad reminder of better times and better fortunes.

I stopped the car.

Franklin's car was parked near the front door. Even

though the driveway was circular, I didn't want Franklin to see me, so I backed up to turn around.

That's when the trouble started, and my stealthy surveillance fell apart.

Baby, seeing Franklin's car and no doubt catching his scent, shot out of the open back window and galloped up to the front door barking when I stopped the car to turn around–you know that little pause you have to make when you put the car from reverse to drive.

Goodness! How was I going to explain this?

Georgie, leaning out the front passenger window, was watching Baby with glee and anticipation. I knew she was thinking of jumping out of the car as well and joining Baby. "Stay, Georgie. Stay!" I quickly closed all the windows as a precaution.

I ran up to the front door–well, limped is more accurate–to gather Baby, but not before the front door flew open.

Of course, Baby shot into the house, looking for Franklin.

And who was standing before me with a stony gaze boring a hole into my soul?

Hunter Wickliffe!

7

Hunter Wickliffe stared at me in surprise, but then gathered his wits. He yelled back into the house, "Oh, Franklin, it seems you have a visitor!"

Franklin ambled to the door with Baby jumping up on him, trying to get attention. "Good Lord, Hunter, she's tracked me here." He pushed Baby down. "Are you stalking me, Josiah?"

Sheepishly, I replied, "I was driving down Old Frankfort Pike and saw you. I thought I would say hi since I was in the neighborhood, so I followed." I peered around Hunter into the house. "So how do you two know each other?"

"This woman has no shame," growled Hunter to Franklin.

I ignored the insult. After all, I did get caught, didn't I? My father always said, "Don't do the crime if you can't do the time."

Looking at the two men, it dawned on me why Hunter Wickliffe looked so familiar when I first met him. He and Franklin must be blood relatives. They had the same lean body, eyes, and hair coloring except Hunter was starting to gray around the temples. "You're Franklin's father!" I blurted out.

Turning to Franklin, I scolded, "I thought you said he was dead."

"Our father did die recently," Hunter replied icily. "That's why I'm here. I'm Franklin's older brother."

I think my mouth dropped open. Oh, I know it did. I had to pick it off the ground. "Excuse me, I don't mean to be rude, but you look considerably older."

"But you are rude, Mrs. Reynolds, and may I say invasive. Do you make it a habit of barging onto private property and unleashing your unruly beast?"

I tried to apologize, but the words stuck in my throat.

Obviously irritated, Hunter snapped, "If you must know, my bratty kid brother was a midlife baby. By the time Franklin was four, I had graduated from college and was living in London. Of course, he delighted my mother to no end."

Franklin chimed in, "Hunter always said Mother had little sense. That's because he was jealous, since she favored me."

"Oh, pipe down, Franklin. We all know you were a mistake. Mother tolerated you, but it was me she adored."

Franklin winked at me. Obviously, the brothers enjoyed taunting each other.

Hunter announced, "Well, there's no point standing around. Come in. Your dog is welcomed as well."

Folks usually shy away from Baby, if not from his size, then from his slobber. Hunter was one of those rare individuals who understood Mastiffs.

"Oh, that reminds me. Georgie is still in the car."

"Who's Georgie?" Franklin asked, looking at the Prius.

Hunter said, "I think she's that little yip-yip furball jumping up and down in the front seat."

Franklin offered, "I'll get her. Have Hunter give you a tour."

"You heard my bratty brother. Come in."

Hunter and I traveled down the main hallway, which divided the house equally on both sides until we reached the kitchen.

Baby followed, excited to sniff new smells.

Hunter retrieved two stainless steel bowls out of an antique pie safe, and after filling them with water, put them on the floor. Grabbing a dishtowel from a chipped white farm sink, he wiped drool dangling in long threads from Baby's mouth.

I had never seen a stranger do that with Baby.

My dog was very particular as to who wiped his drool away, because his muzzle was very sensitive, but Baby didn't seem to mind Hunter messing with him. "There you are, boy. All nice and clean."

Georgie scampered into the kitchen barely missing Baby, who was already slurping water from one of the bowls. She helped herself to the other bowl, making sure she did not get in Baby's way.

I looked around the kitchen. The walls were lined with aged white subway tiles. All the appliances were ancient, but state-of-the-art at the time of purchase. "This place is like a time capsule," I mused.

Hunter pulled a chair out from a battered wooden harvest table and beckoned me to sit.

I was grateful. Running my hand across the old wood, I discovered deep nicks, like someone had taken a knife and started to carve their initials before being caught. Maybe someone like a mischievous little boy. "Did you recently purchase this place?" I inquired.

Hunter yelled down the hallway at Franklin to take the dogs out to relieve themselves.

"He's always barking orders. Just as bad as my dad," commented Franklin, strolling through the kitchen to gather the dogs. They happily followed him outside after Franklin produced a ball from behind his back.

Hunter chuckled as he watched Franklin play with the dogs through the open kitchen door.

"I asked you if you had recently purchased this estate?" I asked again.

Hunter turned to face me. "I heard you the first time. Would you like something to drink? I have beer, iced tea, or tap water."

"Tea would be lovely."

Hunter claimed a tumbler from one of the glass-paned cabinets and poured tea from a pitcher resting on a white marble counter. After he handed me the tumbler, he reached into the refrigerator and snatched a bottle of beer, which he opened with a bottle opener hanging by the sink.

"Sugar?" he inquired.

"This is fine. Thank you."

"You were asking about the house."

"Yes."

"It has been the family home for over seven generations."

"Franklin has never mentioned it. Why doesn't he live here? It's a little run-down, but livable."

"My esteemed brother thinks the house was built on a foundation of sin and will have nothing to do with it."

"By the looks of the house, I would say it was built pre-Civil War."

"Eighteen hundred and thirty-six to be exact."

"Paid for by slave labor?"

"Hemp, horse breeding, and slaves. The triple crown of Kentucky economy before eighteen hundred sixty-one."

"Don't forget bourbon."

"My family didn't imbibe. We were Baptists. We thought liquor was immoral."

I nodded. "It looks like this farm needs a little freshening up. You could employ some of the descendants of those slaves. A few greenbacks go a long way toward making bad karma go away, if thrown in the right direction."

"Is that what you do to make up for the past?"

"My mother's ancestor came over here as an indentured servant, and worked seven years to pay off his debt. He slept at the foot of his master's bed and ate the scraps left after meals the entire seven years." I added, "I have his diary. He was an educated man, but they had him slopping pigs and emptying their slosh pots."

Hunter took a sip of his drink before responding. "You're not one of those idiots who thinks he needs to address evil deeds from centuries ago, are you? I thought you had more sense than that."

"In my case, the pronoun would be 'she.'"

He grinned. "Touché."

I continued, "This is Kentucky. The past is never past. The sins of the father do visit upon the children."

"So you're a Bible-thumper too. Didn't see that coming. Perhaps you think I should give the farm back to the Shawnee?"

"No need to get snippy. Just trying to save you some grief. I know from experience the past has a way of rearing up and biting one on the fanny, or in my case, throwing a person off a cliff."

"It must have been very traumatic."

"Yeah. You know, your life doesn't flash before you when you think you're going to die. You just think–ah shit! Pardon my French."

"You have a potty mouth, you know that?"

"Didn't use to, but then I used to have my head buried in the sand. Don't do that now. Too dangerous."

"One of those dames who faces life head-on, huh?"

"Something like that."

"I say let the dead bury the dead and all that goes with them."

I took a sip of my tea and decided to change the subject. "I guess the investigation into my friends, the Sloans, has been concluded. You don't seem to be concerned it might breach professional ethics to have a material witness in your home."

"I may be burning professional ethics a little around the edges, but my part of the investigation is finished. I've turned my report in. I've been paid. As far as I'm concerned, I'm done."

"Would you like to expand on that?"

"Not really."

"Okay."

"Let's talk about something else," Hunter suggested.

"So—where've you been all this time?"

Hunter smiled.

It was a pleasant smile. He had white, even teeth. I could tell his parents had spent a small fortune on an orthodontist when Hunter was a teenager. So many men in Kentucky have bad teeth. It was nice to come across a man who actually brushes his teeth, flosses, and uses mouthwash.

One of my girlfriends, looking for a husband, said to me, "I don't expect much. My only requirements are that he has a steady job and all his teeth. After that, he can be a bank robber for all I care."

You see the pickings are slim for a man after the age of twenty-five. Men in Kentucky are snapped up early because they wear out fast.

Jumping Jehosaphat! Why was I thinking things like that? I was startled when Hunter spoke again. But this time it was to Georgie who was looking at him and whining.

Hunter picked her up and placed the dog on his lap, rubbing her little gray ears.

The dog made a little nest, settling in nicely.

I searched for Baby. He was lying in the open doorway, panting, and looking ready for a nap.

Franklin joined us, holding a glass of iced tea.

"You like dogs," I said. It was more of a question that a statement."

"Hunter has always been good with animals, especially horses. He used to ride in competitions," Franklin commented.

"What kind of competitions?" I asked.

Franklin answered, his eyes crinkling, "Show. His Tennessee Walkers could really do the 'big lick.'"

"Oh," I replied. I never liked that Tennessee Walkers were used in competitions because of soring, a practice which uses chains, weights, and caustic chemicals, creating pain to teach the high-stepping (big lick) of the horse's front legs for the show ring. Although soring had been outlawed, it was still used.

"Put your look of disapproval away. Franklin's pulling your leg. I competed in showjumping."

"Were you any good at it?"

"I have lots of silver trophies and ribbons in the den that say I was."

"Warm or hot bloods?" (Just for your information cold bloods refer to draft horses, hot bloods are Arabian or Thoroughbreds, and warm bloods are breeds in-between.)

"Hanoverians, mostly."

"You don't ride anymore?"

Franklin interjected, "Dad had to sell the horses when he lost a lot of money in the stock market. That's when we began our descent from Bluegrass aristocracy to regular folks. We put the 'ruined' in ruined gentry."

I looked at Hunter for confirmation. I could never tell if Franklin was telling the truth or teasing.

Hunter nodded. "As hard as our father worked, he could never get back to where he had been financially. I think that was the biggest regret of his life besides Mother dying." He looked around the kitchen. "It's sad Franklin doesn't remember how this place looked in its heyday. It was one of the showplaces of the Bluegrass. We even had royalty stay with us during the Kentucky Derby season."

"Please, not that tired old story again. I'm so sick of hearing about the good old days," said Franklin.

Hunter gave Franklin a disapproving stare. "I don't understand why you don't love our family home."

"Things were not the same for me as they were for you, Hunter. You lived in a patrician bubble growing up. Things were not so idyllic for me."

Hunter sighed. "Yeah, you tell it like you lived on Tobacco Road."

Franklin started to retort, but I cut him off. "If you have a few minutes, I would love to see the house. Franklin, will you show me around?"

"Nah, I've got to get back to town. Let Hunter do it. He loves to show off this mausoleum."

I turned to Hunter. "If it's not too much trouble."

"Is your leg feeling better? I noticed it was trembling a little when you came in."

My face must have turned five shades of red. I don't like people mentioning my flaws.

"Great going there, bro. With that, I leave you two to duke it out." Franklin rose and imitating Mohammed Ali in the ring, left.

"I'm sorry," Hunter said. "I'm a doctor coming from a family of doctors. I notice things."

"There's no need to apologize. I'm overly sensitive about my physical limitations. I try not to be, but when people bring them up, it reminds me . . ." I drifted off.

"Franklin sent me all the newspaper clippings of the incident about him getting shot and you going over the cliff."

"Actually, I pushed the attacker, (I didn't like to say Onan's name), but he pulled me with him before I could get away. But if Franklin hadn't conked him over the head with a vase moments earlier, neither one of us would have made it. It was a great moment in his life. He loves to tell the story in bars to get free drinks."

"I'm surprised both of you are doing so well."

"To tell you the truth, I don't remember much about the fall. It's very hazy, but I have terrible dreams where I'm falling. I hate those dreams." I blushed again. "I don't know why I'm telling you this."

"I would say by the way you walk and hold your left arm, you landed on your left side. Major trauma."

I nodded. "I fell forty feet."

"What saved you from dying?"

"I kept hitting tree branches all the way down, which helped break my fall. I should have died. There are times when I wish I had. Haven't learned to cope with the chronic pain. Pain is my big Achilles heel."

"Your hearing aid is almost undetectable. Problems with it?"

"No. It's very comfortable. I usually forget it's in my ear."

"Most people wouldn't see it. I'm trained to notice things, little details about people. Brain damage?"

"A little, here and there."

"It apparently hasn't affected your speech faculties. You're very verbal."

"The fall affected my memory and other things, but let's talk about something more pleasant."

"Sure." Hunter pushed Georgie off his lap and extended his hand. "Let me help you."

I grabbed Hunter's hand so he could pull me up. I rarely let anyone do that. Hunter Wickliffe did have a way with dogs, horses, and acerbic, bitter invalids, I guess.

"We'll start with the upstairs. Don't worry. Dad had a lift installed for Mother when she became ill."

I noticed Hunter used the British term "lift" for an elevator. They also use torch for flashlight and solicitor for lawyer. "Your parents couldn't have been too poor if they could install an elevator."

"I didn't say we were poor. I said my father could never get back financially to where he had been before he lost money in the stock market. We had been stinking rich. Now we're merely comfortable." Hunter grinned, his eyes sparkling.

So Hunter liked to tease like Franklin. Must be a family trait.

"How did the farm get so run-down?"

"It takes a lot of money to run a farm this size, and someone on the site who wants to put in the effort. My father got on in years, and Franklin was not interested in helping. He hates the country. I was overseas, and then lived in Washington where the job took up all my time. I couldn't get back to see to things like I wanted. When my father took ill, he was in a nursing home for a long time. This place sat empty for years before I decided to come home. It was time."

"All Southerners come home, even if it's in a pine box."

"Huh?"

"It's a Truman Capote quote."

"Pretty accurate I would say. Well, there are more tidbits to the story, but that's basically it."

"Where is Mrs. Wickliffe?"

"There have been two Mrs. Wickliffes."

"Oh," I said, raising an eyebrow or two.

"Both are happily married to other people now."

"Sorry, none of my business."

"Then why did you ask?"

I laughed. "Didn't Franklin tell you? I'm really, really nosy."

"I would say you have an active mind." Hunter gave me a hard stare and then broke it off. "Dogs—stay!"

Baby was already asleep, snoring loudly. Georgie kept jumping up, wanting to be carried.

"I think this little mutt likes you," I said.

"She needs to be trained not to jump up on people. This dog's behavior gives me insight into the Sloans."

I didn't mention that my dog jumped on people too. I was trying to break Baby of it, but having limited success. "Speaking of the Sloans."

Hunter rolled his eyes. "I shouldn't have brought them up. My bad. Please, don't ask me again about them. You know I can't say anything."

"Shoot. Never hurts to try," I muttered. "I'm worried about them."

"Worry about them later. One thing at a time, Miss Josiah. One thing at a time. Let's look at the house right now." Beckoning, Hunter led me to a closet, which housed an elevator. "I'll meet you upstairs."

Georgie and I got in the elevator, and I reluctantly pushed a button. "Oh, please God, don't let us get stuck in this old, rust-bucket."

Nothing.

I pushed the button harder.

Loudly protesting with squeaks and groans, the elevator rose to the second floor. I was never so glad to get out of an elevator that was really a coffin. I would be sure to take the stairs upon leaving–sore leg be damned.

For the next forty-five minutes, Hunter showed me his marvelous house. I would have to say, even in its present condition, it was something to behold. The wide-plank floors were solid ash, and the elaborate, carved railing that graced the curved stairwell was polished walnut. The downstairs ceilings were fifteen feet high which, along with the light streaming from all the windows, gave the rooms a light, airy feeling. A marble fireplace was showcased in every room. The same matching marble graced the counters in the kitchen and three bathrooms. Even the bathtubs were carved out of the same marble. That's right. All of it carved out of a single piece of marble.

Catching a glance at a clock on one of the mantels, I gasped. "Oh, my gosh. I was supposed to pick up some trees, and the nursery closes in half an hour." I turned to Hunter. "Thank you for a lovely time. Your house is something special. I wish you the best of luck with it."

I yelled, "Baby, come!" I listened for a few seconds until I heard the clicking of Baby's nails as he plodded toward me. I winced at the thought of him damaging the floors.

Hunter picked up Georgie. "I'll walk you to your car."

We slowly descended the steps of the portico while Hunter pointed out things of interest until we finally reached my car.

The sun was starting to set, ushering in what we call the gloaming.

He opened the back seat door, letting the dogs climb in while I scooted in the front.

Leaning my head out the window, I said, "I want to apologize for my rude behavior when we first met. I wasn't very nice."

"You were nasty because I startled you. Very understandable. I tend to forget I'm back in the South where one is expected to have manners. I should have introduced myself and explained why you and the dogs couldn't be there without yelling first."

"I wouldn't use the word nasty. I wasn't nasty. You were the one who was nasty."

Hunter grinned. "Nice to see you again, Josiah Reynolds. Keep your chin up, kid, and don't take any wood nickels."

With that, Hunter Wickliffe, the seventh master of the Wickliffe estate, walked back into his faded, aristocratic, Southern mansion.

8

I entered the library where Lady Elsmere, aka June Webster of Monkey's Eyebrow, Kentucky, was perched on an elegant settee. Even though it was warm outside, June warmed herself before a fire.

"Geez, it's hot in here," I commented. "Why do you have a fire?"

"I have a slight chill."

I felt alarmed. "You're not sick, are you?"

"Old people's bones get cold. Just you wait."

"That's good. I don't want you to give me any of your old people cooties."

June tittered. "You must be feeling good today if you're so sassy. And I would like to make the comment that I only seem to see you lately when it's time for tea."

"Speaking of tea, I see you have an extra cup."

"Pour yourself."

"Can you pass a plate? I want some of those little cakes. Hey, it looks like Bess fixed some of those cucumber sandwiches I like so much." I picked one up and studied it. "They look so delicate. How does she do it?"

"Petit fours?" June offered.

"Need you ask? Give 'em up."

June studied me. "You do feel good. What happened to cause this sunny disposition after your depraved behavior?"

"Depraved behavior?" I echoed with my mouth full of a chocolate raspberry tart.

"Eunice told Bess, who told me, you cursed in public, and in front of a gentleman. Not like you at all."

I thought back to what Hunter had said. "I was startled, and it slipped out."

"It used to be that only sailors and ax murderers cursed in public."

"Well, excuse me for being such an embarrassment to you, your royal hiney."

"That's the Josiah I know and love so well."

"It's not like I said it in front of a wide-eyed virgin. This guy is a bit long in the tooth."

"Enough of that. Pour a little brandy in my tea, dear."

"Of course," I replied, reaching for the brandy. "You did say brandy and not bourbon."

"Brandy right now. Maybe a little bourbon later on."

"Do you think we're turning into a couple of old lady alcoholics?" I mused.

"You're not. You have other vices," she ruminated.

Did June know about my illegal stash of pain pills?

June continued, "When you get to be my age, you need a stiff drink to get though the day."

"As if your life is so hard."

"You have no idea."

"Say when." I began pouring the brandy into her teacup. "Say when. SAY WHEN!"

"When."

"That's gotta taste awful. Tea and brandy," I said, watching her take a sip.

"It warms my bones. Old people have cold bones."

"So I've heard."

"Where?"

"Just around here and there."

"About?"

"Old people and their chilled bones."

"Are you making fun of me?"

"Me? Make fun of you? Never."

"You're a horror." June leaned forward and swatted my forearm. How could she even lift her hand with the weight of all those diamond-encrusted bracelets?

"Yeah, but you love me."

June started to protest.

I cut in, teasing. "Don't deny it. You do. You know you do."

"Well, here's mud in your eye." June chuckled while raising her teacup up to her lips. She took a gulp. "You're right. This tastes dreadful. Pour the tea out and hit me with some straight brandy."

I did as requested.

Instead of giving me a thank-you, June muttered, "Monster." She looked at me with a crooked grin. "I do love you."

"I love you too, old woman."

We smiled fondly at each other, leaning back in our chairs, enjoying the fire on a warm day, comfortable in our silence. We didn't speak for a very long time.

"What's on your mind, June?"

"I miss Liam. I want him to come home."

"Can he?"

"No one has pressed charges concerning those jewels."

"You mean the jewels he stole from Walter Neff, who stole them from Thaddeus McPherson, who murdered Bunny Witt, not to be confused with the Boston Whitts with a 'h', in order to steal them himself?"

June shook her head. "No one ever proved there were jewels. Teddy McPherson is kookoo for Cocoa Puffs. No one believes him. Apparently, any documentation, such as the old aunt's diary, has gone missing."

"Walter said he found the jewels, and Liam stole them while Walter was having a heart attack."

"Utter nonsense."

"Then how do you explain finding your emerald necklace on your pillow the morning Liam disappeared?"

"Coincidence."

"I thought the Indian government laid claim to the

jewels. They say they have documentation," I said.

"Even so, it would take years to go through the courts to prove ownership, and I doubt Liam would leave a paper trail as to their whereabouts, or even their very existence."

I whistled in appreciation. "So Liam got away with the perfect jewel heist. You have to tip your hat at him."

June sniffed. "The house seems empty without him. L'amour, l'amour. Even at my age the heart wants what the heart wants."

"That's depressing to hear. I was hoping to dispense with the heart and all the headaches that go with it."

"One day, Jo, love is going to show up when you least expect it."

"I've had two big loves in my life, and they both stank. Love to me is like backing into a porcupine."

"You can't tell me you don't miss Jake."

"I miss him terribly, but we were wrong for each other. He was too young, for one thing. He had two little children. As much as I loved him, I didn't want to raise more kids. I'm not fond of children. I can barely tolerate my own child."

"I think if Jake walked back through the door, you would be ecstatic to see him."

"I would, but then what? Just because you love someone doesn't mean they're right for you, or you for them."

"You're not a romantic."

"No, I'm not. I hope love never shows up on my doorstep again."

We sat silently sipping our "tea" for a long time.

Finally, June asked, "What's on your mind? You didn't come over here to drink brandy and discuss love."

"Do you know anything about an old Kentucky family with the name of Wickliffe?"

June placed her cup in the saucer. "Did you finally realize Franklin is of the Wickliffe line?"

"I'm embarrassed to say this, but I never knew Franklin's last name. To me he was always Franklin, like Cher is Cher or Sinatra is just Sinatra."

June gathered her thoughts for a moment before answering. "The Wickliffes are an early Kentucky family. Franklin and his brother Hunter are descendants of the Wickliffe family that immigrated to Kentucky in seventeen eighty-four.

"The most famous Wickliffe was Charles Wickliffe, who served as governor of Kentucky, US Postmaster General, and for two terms as a US congressman. During the Civil War, he sided with the Union."

"And Franklin's branch?"

"They are descendants from one of the Confederate siblings, who managed to hide his wealth when the Civil War came. He adapted very well to the post-war economy and bought up all the surrounding farms. Many Kentuckians could not pay their taxes at the time, so this Wickliffe made out like a bandit in land acquisitions. The family doubled their income from farming by training all their sons to be lawyers, and later, doctors. With the extra income that provided, they bought partnerships in coal mines in western Kentucky and textile factories up north.

"The family remained extremely wealthy until Franklin's old man, Valerius Cave Wickliffe, dabbled in the stock market. Everyone told him not to invest in those particular funds, but I found Valerius to be a person who could successfully evade the truth, even though it was staring him right in the face."

"Hunter told me the family has lost most of their wealth."

June smirked. "A great deal of it, I'm sure." She took a sip of her brandy. "So you've met Hunter. Handsome devil, isn't he?"

"You've never mentioned Hunter or the Wickliffe connection. Why didn't you tell me Franklin was of the Wickliffe line?"

"I might ask why did Franklin conceal it from us? After all, I hadn't seen Franklin since he was a baby. I would never have recognized him. As for Hunter, I hadn't seen him since his college graduation party."

"Hunter told me he went to live in London afterwards."

"I lost contact with the family. I think it was about the time Miriam, their mother, became ill." June had to think for a moment. "Yes, I remember now. Lord Elsmere had died and I decided to come home. I bought this farm, but lived in town for several years because the house was a wreck. I only socialized with the Wickliffes for a year or two before Miriam took sick, so I didn't know them very well. Miriam had the misfortune of having breast cancer. She went downhill very fast."

She continued, "I didn't see them any more after that. The Wickliffes stopped accepting invitations, due to Miriam's illness. She died, and Valerius became immersed in his medical practice and shut himself off socially."

I replied, "Hunter related a similar story about his dad."

June mused, "I must have Hunter over to dinner. He might like to hear stories about his mother. She was a refined woman. It's a shame Miriam died so young. Speaking of dying, what's up with the Sloans?"

"I haven't heard a word," I confessed.

"Ring up Detective Goetz, and get the scoop."

"He retired some time ago."

"But didn't he get a job with the DA?"

"He met a woman and they moved to Florida."

June looked surprised. "Didn't see that coming. Don't you have another contact?"

"Yes, I do, come to think of it."

"You talk to him, and I'll invite Hunter to a dinner party. Between the two of us, we should find something out."

I love it when Lady Elsmere and I conspire.

Most people don't see it coming.

9

I eased into the duct-taped booth at Al's Bar on Sixth and Limestone.

Kelly looked up in surprise. "Josiah!"

"You've been avoiding me, Officer Kelly."

He looked around to see if anyone was listening. "I thought it best to maintain a low profile. My wife doesn't want me to hang around with you."

"Because of Asa?"

Kelly nodded.

"Completely understandable. How's she doing?"

"When things get bad, my wife pours herself a drink, puts on some lipstick, and pulls herself together. Her anger will pass—I hope."

"Would it help if I told her the affair was all Asa's fault?"

"I think the less said about Asa the better."

"I guess you and the family won't be coming over for Thanksgiving this year?"

"Better pass on that."

We sat in silence, ruminating on the sad state of affairs between us.

I got up to leave. "When things cool off, give me a call."

Kelly reached up, tugging on my arm. "Sit. Did you need something?"

Sitting back down, I replied, "I do, but I can't ask you when things between us are not good. Maybe another time."

"Tell me what you need. I don't want this breach between us."

"I don't want to get you in trouble."

Kelly scratched his stubbled chin with impatience. "Just tell me."

"I want to know about the Sloan case."

"It's still under investigation."

"Was the fire officially declared arson?"

"I think so, but they haven't located either of the Sloans."

The disappointment must have shown on my face.

Kelly offered, "Hey, look. I'll ask some of my buddies in the Fire Department. Feel them out. See what they say."

My expression must have brightened, because Kelly's expression softened. "You're always going out on a limb for others. Be careful, Josiah. People don't care that you put yourself at risk for them. Don't let yourself be used."

Kelly's words alarmed me.

He decided to add a codicil. "You're the best, you know that." He pointed a finger at me. "Don't you ever forget it, no matter what others say."

I crossed my heart. "Never. Never and a day."

10

I was at my usual stand at the Farmer's Market on Saturday morning when Officer Kelly strolled up, and purchased honeysuckle soap and two pounds of my Clover honey.

When the other customers browsing at my booth left, Kelly came behind the stand and whispered, "Sandy Sloan took her entire savings out in cash the same day as the fire, and scattered the money all over the house. The firefighters found half-burnt bills in the house and in the yard, where the wind had blown them. They also found clothes that matched the description you gave of what Sandy was wearing that morning. They were folded neatly by the edge of the cliff.

"They have two working theories—Sandy started the fire and then committed suicide by jumping off the cliff, or Toby Sloan caught her setting the house on fire and killed her in a fit of rage, throwing the body off the cliff, staging it to look like a suicide. Either way, your friend Sandy Sloan is presumed dead."

"But a body hasn't been found?" I was hoping against hope.

"They sent divers into the river, but Josiah, you know how the Kentucky River is. The body could pop up tomorrow or a month from now. I know you hate to hear this, but your friend is probably snagged under a fallen tree somewhere along the river bank."

I clutched my stomach, feeling nauseous. "Thanks. I appreciate the information. One more question—where is Toby?"

"Probably on the lam. No one has seen him or his truck since the morning of the fire. Sorry for the bad news. Wish it could have been better." Kelly shifted his bag of goodies from the market and gave a short nod before leaving.

I looked down at Georgie, who had come to the Market with me. She was wagging her shaggy tail, her golden-brown eyes looking up apprehensively.

"Don't worry, Georgie. He didn't mention anything about Sandy's car. It's not at the house, so Sandy's not dead. She'll come back. You wait and see."

At that moment, I knew I was going to hell. I had sunk to one of the lowest rungs on the skunk ladder. I had lied to a dog.

11

"Now, listen! You are going to do this gratis, you freeloader!" I yelled at Walter Neff.

"No, I'm not. These are my fees. Take 'em or leave 'em."

I was flabbergasted. "You have mooched off me for months, eating my food, having me wait on you while you commandeered my couch, frustrating Eunice to no end, and you have the nerve to tell me that you will only take this case if I pay. I can't believe your gall."

"I don't do cases for free. If you want me to investigate your friend, then you will have to pay. It's professional ethics."

"You don't even know what the word ethics means."

"Sticks and stones, Toots. Sticks and stones."

I took a step toward Walter with the intention of twisting his bulbous nose when suddenly a better idea popped into my head. "Okay, Walter. Be that way. If you won't help me, I'll call Asa and have her come home."

Walter's face blanched. He grabbed my wrist as I reached for the phone. "Let's not be hasty. I'm sure we can work something out. Did I say my regular fee? I meant half."

I brushed off his grimy little hand and picked up the phone. "No deal, schlemiel."

He wrenched the phone away.

"Walter, give me that phone, or I'm going to pick up the nearest blunt object and brain you."

He laughed, dancing around as long as the phone cord on my old-fashioned landline phone would allow.

"Baby, attack. Attack Baby, attack!" I shouted.

Baby lifted his head from between his paws and looked toward Walter. Deciding Walter didn't pose a threat, Baby rolled over on his side, asleep before his head hit the Navajo rug he was lying on.

"Even Baby doesn't take you seriously, Toots," taunted Walter. He proceeded to yank the phone cord from the wall, holding the phone up like some wild game trophy he had just killed.

"Shut up, Neff. You give me a migraine headache. No, I take that back. You are a headache."

"Ooh. That really cuts to the quick. Did you stay up all night thinking of that lame quip?"

"I still have my cell phone in the car. I'm going to march out there and call Asa now. The first thing she'll do is commandeer your Avanti, and haul it off to the junk yard to be crushed into a cube the size of a coffee bean with you in it."

Alarmed, Walter cut in, "Come on, Toots. I was just kidding. There's no need to call Asa." He started toward me.

In a flash, Baby shot up and stood between us, growling at Walter. I reached down and petted Baby's massive head, glad I could always count on him. He was not the obnoxious hairball everyone complained about. He was my protector, my four-legged guardian angel who happened to eat, poop, belch, fart, and shed a lot. Well, nobody's perfect!

Walter slowly backed away, put the phone back on the end table and sat down. "Call him off, Toots. That creature weighs a ton. He could crush me."

"Gee, that would be a shame." I kissed the top of Baby's head. "Good dog, Baby. Good dog. It's okay. Go back to sleep."

Baby gave me a cursory glance, and seeing I was not in danger (as if I ever was from Walter Neff), padded to his bed in the corner of the great room, his good eye still fixed on Walter. Tee-hee. Tee-hee.

"Okay. Okay. You win. Give me the details," sighed Walter.

I passed him a pad and pencil. "I want to find out if Sandy or Toby Sloan are still alive."

Walter sneered, "Is that all?"

"Come on. You claim to be a first-rate shamus. Do your job."

"Will you at least pay my expenses?"

"As long as you bring me the receipts. No receipts— no moolah. Capiche?"

"Capiche."
Walter and I shook on it.
I felt better than I had in a long time.
How was I to know that feeling would not last long?

12

The phone rang, but I didn't recognize the caller ID, so I let the answering machine pick it up.

"Hello? Josiah? This is Hunter Wickliffe. I've been invited–or summoned, I'm not sure which–to dinner at Lady Elsmere's. Haven't seen her in decades, so I don't know why she wants to see me all of a sudden. I was told I could bring a guest, so I'm wondering if you would like to join me. Let me know fast. Dinner is two days from now."

BEEP!

Without any hesitation, I hit the delete button on the answering machine.

There was no way I was going to get tangled up with Wickliffe the way I did with Teddy McPherson.

You know how that turned out–baaaad.

13

I caught sight of Franklin coming across the field as I was putting water out for the honeybees. They drink large amounts of water during the summer to keep the hive cool.

I had scattered around several shallow pans lined with rocks, over which I poured clean water. The rocks were for the bees to land on. Otherwise, they would drown, since they cannot land on water. I used to have a water tank for them but it rusted out, so this had to do until I could purchase a new one.

Franklin sat in my golf cart and waited patiently until I finished.

"Did you walk from Matt's house?"

"Yep."

"Have you told Matt about Hunter yet?"

"Getting around to it, but speaking of Hunter."

"I'd rather not."

"Why haven't you returned his call?"

"You know about that, huh?"

"He's been waiting for you to respond."

"Why do you care if I go out to dinner with him? You don't claim Hunter as your brother. You admitted you haven't told Matt yet."

"I did tell you I had a brother."

"Yeah, but it was the invisible brother. Why haven't you told anyone the prodigal brother had returned?"

"We had to work through some things first."

"Like what?" I asked, waving away a curious bee. (My friends—you should never swat a honeybee. It releases chemicals signaling to other honeybees to join the party. Then you swat more bees, and next you're suddenly the victim of multiple stings. Of course, I swat them all the time. I don't even notice I'm doing it—just like arguing with Franklin.)

Franklin jumped out of the golf cart as more bees began flitting around my head. (See what I mean.) "Regardless of what you think, Josiah, I love my brother. I don't like seeing him treated shabbily. Please call him."

It was rare of Franklin to chastise me and mean it.

Sometimes I think I'm a bad person. I had lied to a dog, and now I had dissed Franklin's big brother. Where was my malice going to end?

"I erased the message with his phone number. Would you call Hunter and tell him I'll meet him at Lady Elsmere's at seven?"

Franklin's face relaxed until it was almost smiling—not quite, but almost. "Yeah, I can help you out there."

"Is it an informal dinner, or shall I bathe?" I quipped.

Ignoring my sarcasm, Franklin said, "Wear your black funeral dress with a strand of pearls. Do you have time to wash your hair? Please make the time. It needs it."

"I don't have time to wash my hair, shave my armpits, or have a bikini wax. I'll take a shower, put on clean underwear without holes, and slap on some lipstick. That's the best I can do."

Franklin gave me the once-over. "You should know Hunter has always gone out with the most beautiful women."

"Well, kiss my granny fanny, Franklin. He called me. I didn't ask him. Now scoot. I've got more work to finish before I can get cleaned up for this folderol."

He pointed at finger at me before walking off. "Be nice to my brother, Jo."

"He's a middle-aged man who doesn't need anyone's protection!" I yelled. "He'd better be nice to me. And by the way, quit giving out the code to my gate." I gave Franklin a raspberry before returning to work.

All my sympathy had faded.

What did Franklin think I was going to do to his brother—ravish him?

I barely had enough energy tonight to look for some pantyhose. Ah, jumping Jehosaphat! It was too hot for hose. I'd go without them. Underwear would be enough, assuming I had any underwear.

Otherwise, au natural it would be, hoping my dress didn't get caught in the universal crack.

Fuming, I watched Franklin walk out of the field.

What nerve!

Like his brother was such a catch!

Why was I thinking that?

14

I was about to leave the house when the doorbell rang. Before I could look at my monitors, Walter opened the front door. I heard a surprised "Hello? Is Josiah available?"

Hurrying into the foyer, I pushed Walter aside. "Hello, Hunter. You didn't have to come to the Butterfly. I was supposed to meet you at Lady Elsmere's."

"Franklin explained that to me, but I'm the old-fashioned sort. You don't mind, do you?"

I gathered my wrap lying on a wormwood table. "I don't if you don't."

Walter whined, "You're going out on a shindig, and I'm stuck here by my lonesome. What am I supposed to do for dinner?"

"There is a whole fridge full of food, plus a walk-in freezer. You'll find something. And don't eat anything

Eunice has marked. Those are for her upcoming events."

Baby and Georgie bounded into the foyer, realizing something was up.

I quickly stepped outside and shut the door. The last thing I wanted was Georgie's fur and Baby's slobber on my dress.

Hunter pointed to the red car parked my driveway. "Whose Avanti?"

"That little gem belongs to Walter Neff."

"The gentleman who opened the door?"

"He is, but he's no gentleman."

"Is he your boyfriend?"

I guffawed. "He's more like the houseguest from hell."

Hunter gave me an odd look.

"He's an acquaintance who's been ill and staying at my house until he recuperates."

"He looks in perfectly good health to me."

"That's what I keep telling him," I sighed. "Enough about Walter. Speaking of cars, that's quite a gem you drove here."

I was looking at a 1980 Rolls-Royce Silver Spur with an off-white interior, which accented the real mahogany dash and sideboards. The coolness ended there.

The paint job was dull and scratched, with rust pushing through the metal. It didn't help the finish that it now had a thin coat of dust from my gravel driveway and one of my peacocks was on the hood leaving a messy gift for Hunter. Oh, dear.

A side mirror was missing as well as the antenna, and two of the whitewall tires had been replaced with common black tires.

Admiring the sleek lines of the car, I said, "This poor baby needs to go to the car hospital."

After shooing the peacock off his car, Hunter opened the passenger door for me. "It's my father's last grand gesture. He bought it for my mother. I don't have the heart to sell it."

"Is that an original Spirit of Ecstasy?" I was referring to the hood ornament gracing all Rolls-Royces, a woman leaning forward with her robes flying back in the wind, resembling wings.

In the early production of Rolls, they did not have a hood ornament, but one of the first purchasers, Britain's Lord Montagu, wanted a custom-made one for his car. He commissioned the sculptor Charles Sykes to sculpt a personal mascot for the hood of his 1910 Rolls-Royce Silver Ghost.

Sykes chose Lord Montagu's mistress, Eleanor Thornton, as the model. Rolls-Royce later asked Sykes to produce an official ornament to be used on all Rolls-Royce cars. He modified his original design based on Eleanor Thornton, and thus the Spirit of Ecstasy was born and became an iconic adornment for all the Rolls-Royces.

As for Miss Thornton, she died when her ship, the SS Persia, was torpedoed in 1915, during WWI, off the coast of Crete. She was accompanying Lord Montagu to his new war assignment.

He survived.

I wonder what Lord Montagu thought later when he saw a Rolls-Royce pass him on the road with a hood ornament modeled on the great love of his life.

I caressed the ornament. Hmm, maybe caress was a bad choice of words, considering her history and name. "This one looks like an older model," I mused.

"There have been several adaptations of her," said Hunter, admiring his Spirit of Ecstasy. "Someone stole the original one decades ago. I found this one in a junk shop in England and brought it back with me.

"Is she sterling silver?"

"Silver-plated."

"Ah." I moved about the car. "The bones are still good. Just needs a freshening here and there."

"Like we all do from time to time."

"I'll say amen to that." I sat in the passenger side, and the door made a creaking noise as Hunter closed it.

The car had a thick, musty odor. I supposed it had been sitting in a barn for years. I hoped mold hadn't taken hold.

Hunter got in and, as if reading my thoughts, said, "I've had her thoroughly cleaned. Don't worry about what you're sitting on."

"I think it's too early in the evening to be mentioning where my posterior is resting. I hardly know you," I teased.

He took a deep breath.

"You seem nervous."

Hunter nodded. "Being summoned by Lady Elsmere makes me feel like I'm being sent for by the school principal. No matter what the reason, it's always nerve-racking." He started the Rolls-Royce, which coughed and sputtered. Finally, the engine roared to life. "Let's get this over with, shall we?"

"Yes, let's." I couldn't have agreed more.

15

It was one of those hot, humid days we have in Kentucky. I was sweating up a storm tending to my animals. I had sheep as well as peafowl, goats, a llama here and there, donkeys, cats, and my three retired Thoroughbreds, which I had saved from the glue factory. They mostly roamed free and foraged, but I liked to periodically count heads, making sure everyone was fine.

Then there were the wild animals, including turkeys, deer, skunks, possums, rabbits, squirrels, coyotes, groundhogs, and a multitude of birds plus my bees.

I also checked the pristine Bluegrass pastures where the boarded horses grazed. I wasn't responsible for their daily care, but I liked to sneak them an apple or two, except for Comanche, Shaneika's racehorse. He always tried to bite me.

Besides the task of feeding and watering my babies, I also cleaned up their messes–manure, in other words.

If I saw a pile in the driveway, I would stop my golf cart and shovel the pie (hopefully hardened) into buckets in the back, which would be taken to a compost pile.

Baby and Georgie tagged along, but were panting heavily. They needed to reduce their temperature.

"We could do with a break," I said to them. Only Georgie looked at me when I spoke. Baby's panting was heavy and labored. Worried that Baby might suffer a heat stroke if he didn't cool off soon, I turned onto Lady Elsmere's property and drove on the road that wound down to the river.

I parked the cart at the top of a knoll. "Come on," I called as I climbed out of the cart.

The dogs followed me down the path to the water with Georgie yapping the entire way. I grabbed the key to the pontoon boat from its hiding place in the sycamore tree.

The air was already cooler by the river, and the dogs and I breathed easier.

"Everyone tinkle," I advised. "We don't want to have any accidents on Lady Elsmere's boat, do we?"

The dogs did as bidden before joining me on the boat. I closed the gate and started the engine. "Here we go. Fasten your seatbelts."

Neither dog thought I was funny. Baby lay down, while Georgie stood by the railing barking at anything that moved.

We turned left toward Fort Boonesborough near Winchester and slowly putt-putted up the river until we came to a little sandy beach. Stopping the boat, I opened the gate and attached a ramp.

Georgie, Baby, and I had no problem walking onto the sandy bank. The dogs immediately ran into the water, splashing happily.

Beaches are rare along the Kentucky River, but once in awhile you might find a sandbar. This was a favorite one of mine. The water was shallow, but still I didn't want the dogs to wander into the deep part of the river and start floating with the current, because the river could be thirty feet deep or more in the center. (Before the locks were installed, a person could walk ankle-deep all the way across the river in certain areas during the summer.)

I waded into the water and, grabbing both their collars, towed the dogs closer to the shore.

Finding the old ragged folding chair which I had left at the beach several years ago, I pulled it over to the edge of the water and sat with my feet in the river.

Baby and Georgie lay near me, enjoying the cool water as well.

The river was quiet except for fish splashing and song birds twittering along the riverbanks. The lazy resonance of a tractor mowing hay in the distance echoed off the cliff walls, as an occasional breeze rustled through the leaves, creating a slight hissing sound. A hawk, riding the day's heat, spiraled high in the sky.

The pleasant humming of insects as the river flowed along its ancient course, combined with the warm sun on my face, seduced me into drifting off.

I don't know how long I was asleep, but I was jerked awake by almost falling out of the chair. "Goodness. I took a snooze," I said to no one in particular.

As soon as I shook my head clear, I checked on the dogs.

Baby was lying in a shallow pool of water, contently snoring, but Georgie was nowhere to be seen.

"Georgie," I yelled, scrambling out of my chair. "GEORGIE! GEORGIE!" Something caught my attention. I tapped on my hearing aid and listened, swiveling my head toward each new sound. I heard barking in the distance.

Deciding the barking was coming from my right, I began searching as far as I could on the riverbank. "Georgie! Georgie!" I kept calling.

Fallen trees blocked my way, so I waded in the shallow water, hoping a poisonous water moccasin wouldn't clamp onto my ankle. I kept going until there was a yawning drop-off in the water. I had to stop. Debris and a steep, slippery bank prohibited me from climbing upward. With my bum leg, there was no way I could make it.

I had to find that mutt. She was my responsibility.

Jostling brush on the incline caught my attention. I called out and heard heavy panting.

I watched expectantly.

Georgie popped her head up above the weeds.

"Oh, Georgie. I thought I had lost you," I admitted, almost crying from relief.

Making a clapping noise, I coaxed, "Come on, Georgie. Follow me. Follow me. That's it. That's it. Come on." I started making my way back to the beach, turning every so often to make sure Georgie was following.

She trailed at a slow pace, seemingly preoccupied with something. I was able to glimpse that she was dragging an object almost as large as she was. The little canine was determined not to leave her treasure behind.

Finally, we both came to an otter slide. I stood at the bottom with my arms out wide. "Jump, Georgie. Jump!"

The tiny, furry dog dropped her object reluctantly, and jumped straight into my arms. I kissed her filthy head while wiping the mud off her paws. Carefully I made my way back to the beach, where I washed Georgie's paws in the river.

Waking Baby (thanks for all your help, Baby), I put the two dogs back on the pontoon, locking the gate so they couldn't get out and follow me.

I hurried back to the otter slide where Georgie's prize had slipped half way down the muddy bank. Grabbing a long branch, I coaxed it down until I could lean over and grab it.

What was it?

Whatever it was, it had a horrible smell.

I picked up a smaller branch, wiping off the mud caked on it the object.

Lord. I could barely stand the stink.

The mud fell off in clumps, and I stared at something I knew well. I stumbled back into the river in horror, almost falling. The stinky object was a cowboy boot, and not just any boot. I immediately recognized it as one of Toby Sloan's boots, the ones he wore to work every day.

Stifling a retch, I peered inside the boot. That's when I lost it and vomited in the Kentucky River.

Inside the boot was a ragged decomposing foot.

Toby Sloan's foot!

16

After taking my statement, the police made me leave. They wouldn't even let me observe at a distance from the pontoon boat.

I took the boat back to the dock, where Charles was waiting for me with the Land Rover. I wasn't surprised to see him. Lady Elsmere knows everything that goes on.

I moored the boat and let the dogs off. They ran up to the car, sniffing the tires.

Charles met me on the dock.

I handed him the key to the pontoon. "Is she in the car?"

"Yes, Josiah. Lady Elsmere wanted to make sure you reached home safely."

"Thanks. I appreciate it."

"Let me secure the boat, and I'll drive you back."

I nodded and then toddled up to the Land Rover. Opening the front passenger door, I called to the dogs, "Here babies. Here." Both dogs jumped in the front seat.

Exhausted, I climbed in the back next to Lady Elsmere.

"Was it Toby's?" asked June.

I clutched her arm. "I'm afraid so. It looked exactly like the boots he always wore."

"And there was a foot inside?"

"It was horrible." I held my stomach as though I might vomit again. "Georgie found it."

"Poor Georgie."

"What's going on? The cops wouldn't let me stay."

"The police have closed down Tates Creek Road. They're working upriver from the ferry landing, combing the riverbank for the rest of the body. Divers are coming first thing tomorrow morning."

"Do you think it was a suicide?" I asked.

"I think anything is possible. Previously, the divers looked for Sandy west of her house, following the current. Now they're investigating all the way up to the Boonesborough lock, since Toby was found east of here."

"I'm worried they're both dead."

June asked, "Why do you say that?"

"It makes sense that Toby came home to find Sandy setting fire to the house and burning their life savings. He threw her off the cliff in a fit of rage, making it look like suicide. Then he killed himself in remorse," I suggested.

"Possibly. Possibly not. Remember that Sandy's clothes were neatly folded beside the cliff. If a woman thinks she's going to be thrown off a cliff, she's not going to neatly fold her clothes. She would have struggled, and there was no sign of that."

"How do you know?"

"I have my sources. When you went over to the house with Eunice, did you see any signs of a struggle?"

"I didn't go near the edge of the cliff."

"Well, there were none, and a man would have time to cool down if he's making someone take off their clothes and allowing them to be neatly folded. Besides, where is Sandy's minivan?"

"Toby hid it somewhere. Maybe Toby had been planning this a long time. Maybe he forced Sandy to take out their money, set the house on fire, and then killed her so he could be with his sweetie. After all, we don't know how much money we're talking about here. Maybe just a little of the money was burned in the fire, and the rest is of it is safely hidden away. "

"There's one thing wrong with your theory, Josiah."

"What's that?"

"Toby's dead, and no one has found Sandy, alive or dead."

I slumped against the car seat.

"This has been a strange and shocking tale. That's why you'll find dinner ready at your house. All you need to do is eat and go to bed. You need rest. Charles will take the dogs for the night."

"I'd rather have them with me," I said. "They're a comfort."

"As you wish. At least let Charles hose them down before you take them into the house. They're filthy."

"That would be nice." I spied my golf cart. "What about my cart?"

June reassured me. "I'll have one of the grandsons drive it back to your house. Don't worry."

Charles squeezed into the driver's seat, pushing Baby's huge head out of his way. "The Butterfly, Lady Elsmere?"

June answered, "Yes, Charles. I think our Jo needs a nap."

"Tell Bess thanks for the dinner, Charles. I was going to fix some toast and hot tea," I said.

Charles glanced in the rearview mirror and grunted an acknowledgement while starting the Land Rover.

It wasn't long before I was inside the Butterfly with two wet but ravenous dogs. I had helped Charles clean them with June giving backseat instructions on how to hose them properly. Before they left, Charles let in the Kitty Kaboodle before checking all the doors and windows, making sure they were locked. Satisfied I was safe for the night, Charles drove June back to the Big House.

Looking around my home, I felt safe.

But was I really?

Toby Sloan hadn't been safe in his home.

Neither had Sandy.

Was she dead too?

Would the divers find her snagged under a tree along the river as Kelly suggested?

My mind raced through different scenarios.

Why would Sandy take out money only to burn it?

Why would anyone burn their life savings?

That was crazy.

Was Sandy crazy? Is Sandy crazy?

Maybe she had attacked Toby and killed him, using the fire to hide her crime. Then why was Toby's body found miles upriver? The current ran in the opposite direction. He wouldn't have drifted east. And where was Toby's pickup truck?

The divers had already searched the river around the Sandy's house and found nothing.

Maybe she tried to stab Toby again with a butcher knife, and Toby killed Sandy in self-defense, hiding her body in the river near Fort Boonesborough. Then he had killed himself in remorse.

Thinking of all the possibilities made my head ache.

I put Georgie on my bed so we could huddle together. The cats soon joined us, with one making a nest at the top of my head. The rest fell asleep at the foot of the bed near my feet.

Baby stretched out alongside my bed, while Georgie settled on the pillow next to me with her nose close to my ear. I listened to her breathing. I didn't need a hearing aid to hear every inhale and exhale.

It had been a stressful day for all three of us. It was time to go to sleep.

Thank goodness.

17

I rose early the next morning. Eunice was having a small reception on the patio around the pool, so I needed to help. I dressed in respectable black, pinned my red hair back (looked to see if it needed a touch-up–not yet), and put on some makeup.

As usual, both dogs sat in the bathroom doorway watching my every movement. I have no privacy, but I'm not complaining. After yesterday, the presence of others was a comfort.

Hearing noise outside my bedroom, I knew Eunice was already here and giving instructions to the workmen. To be sure, I looked through the peephole on my steel bedroom door and saw her moving about.

Safe.

As soon as I opened the door, the dogs made a beeline to the kitchen, where breakfast awaited. I hobbled after them.

"Josiah, what are you going to do with these dogs?" yelled Eunice, seemingly exasperated, which wasn't like her at all.

Opening several cans of dog food, I replied, "You know the drill. After they've eaten, I will take them to Charles, who will put them in a horse stall with the meanest, most vicious stallion on the farm."

"Ha, ha. Not funny."

I put two bowls down, and hopped out of the way in a hurry before I was run over by Baby. "I'll take them to Charles like I always do, Eunice. They have to eat first."

"Why can't Charles feed them?"

I pointed to Baby. "Look, he's already finished. It just takes a minute. Why are you so jumpy?"

"The police have blocked off the road, and some of the workers are late, as well as the rental tables and chairs. The tables should have been set up by now."

She directed a stern look at Georgie who was looking up at her, wagging her tail. "I wouldn't have this problem if this dog hadn't found–oh, it's so disgusting, I can hardly think about it."

Wow! News gets around fast. I guess the police told Eunice about the decomposed foot when she passed the blockade coming to work. No wonder she was agitated.

I put my hand on Eunice's shoulder, trying to reassure her. Can you believe I'm the voice of reason here? "I'm taking them now. As soon as I drop them off, I will be back to help."

Eunice gave me the look—you know, the look people give which indicates you are less than useful.

"Well, I declare. That's insulting," I protested.

"You can help by going to where the police have cordoned off the road, and tell them which trucks are to be let through."

"I can do that."

"But don't take the golf cart. I need it."

Apparently, June had the grandsons deliver the cart early this morning. She always had my back.

"Okay. We're going now."

"Don't come back till three-thirty."

I snapped my heels together and gave the Roman salute. "Yes, Caesar."

"GO!"

I was being thrown out of my own house, but since my cut of today's reception would allow me to start work on installing water to a field needed for pasture, I capitulated. Without Eunice, I would be in the red every year.

Most of my private income went to pay medical bills. The money I made with Eunice allowed me to get my hair done, have a pedicure every now and then, and keep up the farm.

So when Eunice told me to get out, I vamoosed. "Come on, little doggies." The three of us headed out the side door to my Prius.

I took the shortcut over to June's farm, and found Charles in the tractor shed giving instructions to his grandsons about cutting hay.

As soon as the boys finished cutting and baling hay for June, they would scamper over to my farm and cut hay as well, for which I pay a nominal rental fee for the use of the tractor, gas money, and the boys' wages.

It was a win-win. This arrangement gave the grandsons extra money, and saved me the wear and tear on my own tractor.

I would need the hay for the boarded horses and my animals, come winter. It was essential that only certain fields were mowed, as I left other fields fallow so the bees could forage wild flowers. Those fields wouldn't be cut until later. Ya gotta work with nature, folks.

The boys were careful to look for fawns which might be hiding in the thick grass. If they spotted one, they moved away from its hiding place. They also looked for turkey nests. These boys were good spotters.

I always felt confident the wild animals on my farm would be protected with the Dupuy boys driving the tractors.

Charles and I chatted for a few moments, and then I attempted to leave the dogs with him.

Baby was apt to get into trouble on June's farm, and the farm hands were afraid of him, so Charles always put Baby in a stall with plenty of water and chew toys.

Baby didn't mind. He took the time to catch up on his snoozing, and as long as he had some "chewies," he was fine with the world until I came to collect him.

This was not the case with Georgie. She whined and clawed the stall door as soon as it was shut.

"Charles, I'll take her with me."

"You sure? She'll calm down soon."

"I don't think she will. I'll take her. Georgie won't be a bother. I'm just going up to the spot where the police have blocked off the road."

Looking doubtful, Charles opened the stall door and put a leash on Georgie before letting her out.

Baby was already asleep.

My heart melted. I love big, lazy dogs.

"Thanks, Charles. You don't need to worry about Baby. I'll come by from time to time and check on him."

"You sure?"

"Yes, you go about your business. We'll be fine."

Charles looked doubtful. "Okay, but call me if you need something. I'll be in the office at Barn Three until the early afternoon."

"Scoot."

Charles left grudgingly. His reluctance gave me pause. I guess everyone was on edge since Georgie found Toby's foot.

Georgie and I rushed to where the police had their blockade set up. Just in time, too. The driver of a large delivery van and a policeman were in a heated discussion. I parked the car and hurried over. It took a few moments before it was straightened out, but Eunice's tables were finally on their way.

I went back to my car, and must have dozed off when someone tapped me on the shoulder. Startled, I began fending off the "intruder."

"Hey, watch it!"

I straightened up in the seat, only to have Georgie jump in my lap, sticking her head out the window, pounding my chest with her happy tail. "What are you doing here?" I asked Hunter Wickliffe.

"I got a call. Sounds like someone found a decomposed body."

"A foot in a boot."

"How do you know?"

"Because I'm the someone who found it, or rather Georgie did."

"Hmm, bet that was rather nasty."

"Rather." I put on my sunglasses. "I thought you were off the case."

"I am, officially. I was asked to come unofficially."

"You can do that?"

"Sometimes." Hunter peered into the backseat. "Where's the big dog?"

"Baby."

"Excuse me?"

"Baby is the name of my dog."

"I remember."

I shot Hunter a doubtful look. "He's in prison."

Hunter frowned.

I added, "Baby doesn't do well with a lot of strange people. He likes to terrorize them by sticking his snoot in their cahoots. The men are especially prone to high-pitched indignation when it happens."

"He takes after you then."

"I beg your pardon. I don't put my snoot in other people's cahoots."

"No, but you like catching people off guard."

"Like when?"

"Like that dreadful dinner with Lady Elsmere."

"I had nothing to do with it. I was as surprised as you."

"There I was in my best suit and you in . . . what was that . . . your official cocktail dress or something?"

I nodded sheepishly. "My funeral dress."

"I had a haircut for the occasion and even put on cologne."

"You did smell good."

"That's not the point. I had no idea dinner was going to be a casual affair, and we were going to be served on chipped plates and drink out of mason jars. Was Lady Elsmere trying to insult me?"

"Oh, goodness, no. Is that what you thought? She was trying to make you feel like part of the family. We should blame Franklin for the folly that night. He told me to wear my black dress, so I thought it was going to be a formal dinner."

"The little snake. He told me to get 'duded' up too."

We both laughed.

"It's Franklin's little joke on us," I chuckled. "Didn't you find the food tasty, at least?"

Hunter nodded. "I have to admit the dinner was good indeed. Very Southern." Hunter ticked off his fingers. "Pulled pork barbeque, stewed tomatoes and okra, fresh peas, baked potatoes, sliced peaches in syrup, homemade coleslaw, johnny cakes, orange pound cake with homemade vanilla ice cream. Very good, but I'm not used to the servants eating with the employer. When did that start to be a thing?"

"Let me explain something. The servants are not servants. Charles Dupuy and his family are to inherit June's estate. They're family."

Hunter's face fell. "I remember now you told me that before. I didn't make the connection. You must think me a jerk."

"You lived in England for a very long time where there is a more rigid class system."

"I thought they were employees taking advantage of an old woman."

"If anyone is being taken advantage of, it's Charles. June drives him nuts." I could tell Hunter was distressed and going over the evening in his mind. "I wouldn't worry about it, Hunter."

"Was I rude? I feel like a horse's ass now."

Trying to assure him, I said, "You were stiff, that's all."

"Maybe I could ask everyone over to my house for a picnic?"

"I think Charles would be very interested to see your house, and I know June would be ecstatic." I changed the subject. "Did you learn anything about your mother from June?"

Without notice, Hunter segued to another subject. It caught me off guard. I wondered if it was because I had mentioned his mother.

"I have to go to a banquet next Thursday. An old acquaintance of mine is getting some sort of an award. I was wondering if you would like to join me?"

"No."

"Just like that?"

"Okay. No, thank you."

"Is it because of that Walter Neff guy?"

"Yes, it is. We are hot and heavy. He's fire between the sheets."

Hunter was completely taken aback. He quickly regained his composure. "You're teasing."

"I'm sure you're a nice man, but I'm not interested in dating anyone now or ever. I'm done with that part of my life."

"I'm not asking you to go steady. I'm new in town. I don't know anyone but you, Franklin, June, and now June's heirs."

"You grew up here. You don't need anyone to show you around."

"When I left, Lexington was a tiny Southern town. Now it's a cosmopolitan city. I heard four languages when I went to the hardware store yesterday."

I shrugged.

"I'm asking you to be my escort for the evening."

"See, that's what I'm talking about. You used the word 'escort.'"

"What's wrong with the word 'escort?'"

"It sounds too sexy. I don't do sex. In fact, I can't ever have sex. I think my hoohoo has been absorbed into my body. It's no longer there."

"Have you checked recently?"

"Every damn day."

"You must be a very repressed woman if you can't even use the words escort or vagina."

"There you go again. Using words that are too sex-oriented."

"I'm a psychiatrist. I am not going to use the word, hoohoo in reference to a woman's private parts. How old are you? You talk like a child."

"Hmm." I crossed my arms.

"I need an escort–excuse me, a friend–to accompany me to this award ceremony, and I'm not taking Franklin. He'd show up dressed as Roy Rogers or in a clown suit. I need a lady who has a respectable black dress and a decent strand of pearls she can wear."

"I'll go on one condition."

"Oh, boy, this is going to be interesting. Shoot."

"Give me information about Toby and Sandy Sloan. I want to know what was in your report."

"You little blackmailer."

"No information. No black dress with pearls."

"I can't tell you what was in my report. That's confidential."

"Have fun going by yourself."

"But I can tell you things I hear through the rumor mill."

I gave Hunter a lopsided smile and batted my eyelashes.

A police cruiser pulled up and honked at Hunter. He turned and waved. "Coming. Coming."

"Pick me up at six. I'll have my hair combed and wear my black funeral dress."

"Don't forget the pearls. It reminds me of Donna Reed and gets me all stirred up. Grrrrrr. Sexy!" Hunter winked.

"Pervert."

He petted Georgie, still in my lap, who was so excited she tinkled some drops on me. Ignoring my damp lap like a gentleman, Hunter bid goodbye and left in the police cruiser.

I didn't think of Hunter Wickliffe again for the rest of the day.

Other things intervened. I spent the next hour chatting up the cop manning the roadblock. He told me lots of tidbits, which I'll tell you later. We both were leaning on the police cruiser gossiping away when the chatter started on the police radio.

Apparently the divers had found the rest of Toby's decomposing body in the river near Winchester.

He had been shot.

I looked at Georgie who was leaning halfway out my car window, wagging her tail.

Poor Georgie.

Oh, poor Toby!

18

The house had been put to rights and the guests had left, as had Eunice and her crew.

I really didn't like having my house rented out for social events, but it paid the bills.

One has to do what one has to do in order to survive.

I went through each room to make sure nothing had been broken or stolen.

I know Eunice had already taken stock before she left, but I felt better after I counted my paintings and touched my glass art, especially my Stephen Powell and Brook White pieces.

I could feel my blood pressure go down as I walked through the Butterfly where the pictures were upright on the concrete walls, the furniture gleaming, and the windows were streak-free. These things might not seem important to you, but they are everything to me. A clean house put right meant the world was safe, thus I was safe.

I checked on Baby and Georgie. Baby was sleeping in my room. Georgie had jumped up on my bed and made herself a little nest from my pillows. Both looked content.

I kept walking around the house. I was restless after hearing about Toby.

When death raises its nasty head, it's so often a surprise, isn't it? Even when you're expecting it, it's a shock to the system.

I felt fidgety—I had to do something. I looked at Sandy's landscape on my walls. I loved her serene depictions of our beautiful Bluegrass region and river. Then it hit me.

Jumping Jehosaphat! Where were all the paintings Sandy had stored at her house? Had they burned in the fire? They were worth a small fortune.

I grabbed my wolf's head cane and hurried out of the house to my golf cart.

In the golf cart, it only took me minutes to take the back path to Sandy and Toby's house. The air surrounding the ruined house still reeked of fumes, scorched lumber, and dashed hopes.

I climbed out and pulled the crime scene tape down. I stood for a while, studying the husk which used to be Sandy's home.

The house was built around 1910. A lot of houses at that time had a back porch off the kitchen, usually screened, which was used as a laundry room as well as for storage. Many a freezer was kept on the back porch.

Sandy had converted hers into a studio. It's also where she stored her paintings.

Fortunately, it was still standing. The fire hadn't come back this far into the house.

Tentatively, I crept up the steps and yanked on the screen door. It creaked and groaned, but finally yielded.

I prodded the floor with my cane. It seemed firm, so I stepped up on the porch, but was careful. I surveyed the room from the back door.

Sandy's easel was there. The fold-up chair where she sat as she painted was there. Her paint box was stored by the back door as was the other gear she took when she went on location to paint outside. Blank canvases, which had been gessoed, were stacked against a wall, but there were no finished paintings.

Where were they?

Had the police taken them?

Had the house been looted?

Had Sandy thrown her paintings into the fire?

Had she even been here when the fire started?

I walked around the back porch, poking at things with my cane, looking for scorched bits of canvas and stretchers.

Nothing.

I sat back in my cart and stared at the house, remembering the happy times I had spent with Sandy, discussing art and helping her stretch canvas. She would bring out some wine and cheese, and before we knew it, the sun had drifted across the river and over the Palisades, casting deep shadows.

What remained of the house seemed to be in mourning. Desolate. All the joy had been sucked out and had disappeared into the wind like a wisp of smoke.

It was time to leave. I started the golf cart and turned it around to go home.

Baby was probably awake and wondering where I was.

As I was tooling down the path, I noticed the door to a smokehouse, belonging to old man Combs, ajar.

I had a sudden hunch.

Mr. Combs was a grouchy old coot who had never liked Sandy or Toby because of a property line dispute. He claimed Toby's equipment shed was on his property.

Toby had the land surveyed and found he was in the right, but Mr. Combs wouldn't accept the results of the survey. He continually chewed on his discontent, always complaining about this and that, until Toby mentioned he might have to take the old man to court to stop his harassment.

I didn't care for Mr. Combs either. He was not a good neighbor. If my animals strayed on his farm, he threatened to shoot them. He was a fussbucket, always sticking his nose where it didn't belong.

Let me tell you a thing or two about Mr. Combs. He was an uneducated miscreant who lived in a rundown house on some of the most valuable property in Kentucky. His grandparents had built the family home, and also the home next door, intended for their unmarried daughter, who later died from consumption in the fifties. They sold off the daughter's house and it passed through various hands until Toby and Sandy purchased it.

I don't think old man Combs ever forgave his grandparents for splitting up the land, but his parents kept their portion of the farm intact for their son.

Combs is a very old Kentucky family name, and the original Kentucky Combs were said to have come over the Cumberland Pass with Daniel Boone, but then all old families lay claim to that. The first Combs to set foot in the New World was a young man by the name of John Combs, who sailed on the Marigold and landed at Jamestown in 1619. His descendants migrated to Kentucky in the late seventeen hundreds.

Mr. Combs felt anyone whose family hadn't lived in Kentucky for more than two hundred years was a newcomer, and not to be trusted.

Combs was such an ornery old fart, if he thought he could put one over on Toby and Sandy, he would.

That's why the partially opened door intrigued me. Combs was a man of strict habits, and always kept the doors to his outbuildings shut–tight as a drum.

I pulled my cart up to the door and climbed out. Wrenching the door open, I peered in.

"Talk about a dog thinkin' he's treed a possum," I muttered.

Stacked against the walls of the smoke house were Sandy's paintings. As quickly as I could, I began putting them in my golf cart–that is until I heard the sound of a pump action shotgun being racked.

You know that awful sound that says someone was aiming to put a load of buckshot into your derriere–or worse.

I slowly turned around.

"Whatcha think you're doin', Miss Josiah?" asked Mr. Combs. He spat a brown stream of tobacco juice on the ground while pointing a Mossberg 500 shotgun at my belly.

"I'm taking Sandy's paintings, Darius." (Yeah, that's right–Darius. His mother had a thing for Persian history.)

"No, you ain't. You're trespassing, and stealing my propitty. I got every right to shoot you right here, string you up, and gut you like a wild pig."

The word "gut" gave me pause, but if I backed down, Darius Combs would always bully me. "Don't be so dramatic. You listen to me, Darius Combs." I pointed a finger at him. "These paintings are not your property."

"Sandy give me them pictures."

I scoffed. "Sandy wouldn't have given you the time of day, let alone her paintings. I'm taking them. If you don't like it, call the police, or take me to court."

"I mean it, girlie. Get them pictures out of your vehicle. I don't chew my cabbage twice."

I scooted into in my cart. "I'm going. You better not shoot me, Darius."

Darius spewed a stream of brown slime again. Yuck! "I'd better not find you on my propitty again. You'd better stay gone, if ya know what's good fer ya."

He didn't have to tell me twice. I put the pedal to the metal and got the hell out of Dodge as fast as my little cart would go. I felt like my back had a big bull's-eye plastered on it.

Luckily, Darius thought better of shooting me. I reached home safely, and quickly stored the paintings in my coat closet, covering them with old blankets. Worn out, I just wanted to take a nap. I'd call Shaneika tomorrow and discuss what to do with the paintings.

Hearing noise, Baby and Georgie found me, both nudging to be petted and fed. I hugged them both. "Baby and Georgie, I want you both to listen to me. I don't want either of you wandering next door. Darius Combs has his feathers ruffled, and no telling what he might do."

Both dogs cocked their heads, trying to understand me. Bless their hearts.

After giving them another hug, I fed them, feeling mighty pleased with myself.

I guess Darius Combs knew by now that I had managed to cart off most of Sandy's paintings.

And I knew he would try to get revenge. Darius Combs was that kind of person.

I pondered for a moment.

If he was mad at Sandy and Toby, had he tried to take revenge by torching their house and killing both of them?

Was he that low-down and mean?

Maybe I shouldn't have stirred up a hornet's nest by taking the paintings, but what was done was done.

I had saved most of Sandy's recent works for her.
If she was still alive.

19

Shaneika had the paintings appraised and insured under Sandy's name. After she called the police about the paintings, she was surprised to find they were not interested in them or Darius Combs. They were working on another angle, but wouldn't tell her who or what they were investigating. So she stored them in a bank storage vault, giving me one of the keys since I had paid for the insurance on them.

We were both coming out of the bank when we ran into Hunter Wickliffe.

"Hello, ladies. Miss Shaneika. Miss Josiah," greeted Hunter, tipping his hat.

We both eyed him suspiciously. *We just happened to run into him?*

He must have recognized the doubtful expressions on our faces, because he tried to explain. "I was going in the bank to make a deposit."

"Unhuh," said Shaneika.

"Really, ladies. This meeting is a coincidence."

"Unhuh," said Shaneika again.

Shaking his head, he said, "You are the two most suspicious women I have ever met."

"I find in my work there is no such thing as coincidence," offered Shaneika. "I'll leave you here, Josiah."

"Great. Abandon me to fend for myself, Shaneika."

"Good day, Mr. Wickliffe," said Shaneika.

"Good day, ma'am," replied Hunter, his jaw tightening. He watched her cross the street and saunter into her office building.

"I don't think Miss Shaneika likes me."

"She doesn't know you well enough to like or dislike," I replied emphatically. "Talk about someone being paranoid. You know what they say about being paranoid."

Hunter interjected, "Doesn't mean someone's not out to get you." He stared at Shaneika's office building.

I could tell the thought bothered Hunter, realizing Hunter believed he had a way with women, and it baffled him that Shaneika was so cold.

Chalk one up for Shaneika Mary Todd. She had thrown a curve ball at Hunter Wickliffe.

"Nice to see you again, Hunter. Have a good day."

Hunter grabbed my arm.

I pulled away sharply.

"Sorry. I forgot you don't like to be touched."

"I don't like to be tugged on. Do you always grab women?"

"I don't always have women walking away from me the way you do. It's frustrating to have a conversation with you. As soon as you say hello, I blink and you're saying goodbye."

"I have an agenda today that doesn't include you. Good day, sir."

"Josiah, please, a few moments."

"Ah, the magic word–please."

"Are we still on for the awards banquet?"

"Do you have any news for me?"

"I might have a tidbit or two which will interest that inquisitive mind of yours."

"Yep."

"Yep what?"

"Yep, I'll go," I answered, feeling more kindly toward Hunter.

"Shall I pick you up?"

"Nope. I'll meet you there. Just email me the address."

"I understand you found some of Sandy's paintings in a neighbor's barn."

"News travels fast."

"A gun was pulled on you?"

"I'm not pressing charges. Darius Combs is a crotchety old man, set in his ways."

"Be careful, Josiah. I have dealt with many a case where an old man's threats were carried out."

"Ah, gee, thanks for the insight. Now I'll really feel paranoid."

"When people threaten, they're not blowing off steam. Most of the time, they mean it."

"I know, Hunter. Why do you think I walk with a limp and wear a hearing aid? Because of idle threats?"

"Just want you to be careful. Is Walter Neff still staying with you?"

"Yes," I lied.

"Good. Very good. Well, I'll let you go. See you in a few days."

"Goodbye, Hunter. I'll be careful. I promise."

On the way home, I thought over what Hunter had said to me. It was unnerving, to say the least.

20

The problem was, I liked Hunter Wickliffe.

He was near my age, handsome but not too handsome, educated, good with animals, kind, and seemingly not a psychopath. But who knows? He might prove me wrong. I've been duped before.

But I don't have the inclination for romance anymore. Since Brannon left, and then Jake, I have felt barren like an old tree losing its leaves.

I had some twenty good years with Brannon before our marriage fell apart. I could have forgiven him for his affair with Ellen Boudreaux

The heart wants what the heart wants.

People have little to say about whom they fall in love with, but stealing my couture dresses, hiding money, and giving my Duveneck painting to his mistress were deliberate acts designed to belittle and wound both Asa and me, not to mention leaving us in the poorhouse. I'll never forgive Brannon for that. And to tell you the truth, I'm glad he's dead, even though I miss him from time to time.

As for sweet Jake, the timing wasn't right, and our ages were too far apart. I will always love Jake and be grateful for everything he did for me. I think of him every day, and wish him well.

But after Jake, I dried up completely. I know my limitations. When Detective Goetz was interested, I couldn't rev up the energy or enthusiasm to meet him halfway. I always had the feeling he kept pursuing me because he felt guilty about Onan. I don't want to be anyone's mercy date. He's a good man, but I knew I wasn't the right fit for him.

When Teddy McPherson was "courting" me, I realized something didn't quite smell right. He was way above my pay grade for a companion, if you know what I mean. My instincts proved me right and kept me from being one of his victims.

Let's not talk about Walter Neff. The very thought of him gives me the shivers, and not in a good way.

My current problem is, I don't see an angle with Hunter. He seems sincere. I guess that's why I give him a hard time. There has to be a flaw somewhere—don't you think?

I went to the awards banquet with Hunter and had a nice time. A very nice time. We had drinks, interesting conversation, and laughs.

For the very first time in years, I had a relaxing and enjoyable evening. I wasn't worried about paying bills, or about my health, or even if some man was going to jump out of the bushes at me.

I lived in the moment.

That's very hard to do for people who have had tragedy thrust upon them. They're always looking around the corner to see what lurks in the dark.

But that night I wasn't apprehensive. I was laughing.

So when Hunter asked me out for the next weekend, I accepted.

When will I learn to look before I leap?

21

Hunter and I had made a date to see a movie at the Kentucky Theater on Main Street in downtown Lexington. We were going to see *Strangers On A Train*, a Hitchcock movie where two men meet on a train accidentally, and each plan to commit murder for the other.

I was to meet Hunter at a nearby watering hole to wash down a quick cocktail before heading over to the theater. Movies always seem better when I'm halfway sloshed.

I walked into the bar and stood near the entrance, letting my eyes adjust to the dim light.

Near the back sat Hunter at a table. He saw me and waved, motioning me back.

I started toward the table.

It was then I noticed a young woman sitting with him.

She turned in her chair toward me as her eyes glittered in triumph.

The woman was Ellen Boudreaux!!

22

I must have stumbled out onto the sidewalk, because the next thing I knew I was sitting on a bench with my head between my legs.

"Take deep breaths," cautioned Hunter, standing beside me patting my back. "Deep breaths. That's it. Good. Good."

I calmed down to where I could sit upright. Slowly I got my bearings as my head cleared.

Hunter asked, "What happened, Josiah? You saw me and flew out of the bar."

"That woman!" I blurted out.

"Miss Boudreaux?"

"What were you doing with her?"

Surprise overtook Hunter's face. "Just having a quick meeting about buying a horse. She's representing her father's stables."

"You just happened to be at the bank when I'm

coming out, and just happened to have a meeting with Ellen Boudreaux when we are to meet. You stupid man! Do you take me for a fool?"

Hunter gave me a steely look with his liquid brown eyes. "Even for you, that's unkind."

"If I'm so horrible, why did you bother to ask me out?"

"I'm beginning to wonder."

I stood up rather hastily and wobbled.

Hunter reached over to steady me.

"Don't touch me! Just don't," I cried.

Hunter stepped back and watched me cross the street to my car.

He was still watching, shaking his head, as I drove away.

23

"You're crazy, you know that?" chastised Franklin, putting a cloth filled with ice on my forehead. "Made a complete fool of yourself."

"I know. I know." I opened my eyes to find Baby, Georgie, several cats, and Franklin glaring at me with concern, irritation, and love. I don't need to tell who had which expression. I think you know. "How did you find out?"

"Hunter called. He wanted me to check on you. He said your behavior wasn't rational."

"Oh," was all I replied.

"Of course, Ellen Boudreaux has spread it all over town that you've lost your mind."

"Oh," I moaned again while throwing a pillow across my face.

Franklin asked, "What's that, crazy woman? I can't hear you." He tugged the pillow away.

Sitting up, I whined, "I acted like a complete fool, but your brother set me up. I was stunned to see Ellen with him–and I lost it."

"My brother did not set you up. He had no idea who Ellen Boudreaux was to you. The meeting about buying a horse was legit. I think Ellen saw an opportunity to stick a thorn in your side, and took advantage of it without Hunter's knowledge. Everyone in town knows you two are dating."

"We are not dating," I explained. "I'm showing him around town, that's all. Oh crap!"

"What now?"

"Some ice went down my back. Merde. Merde."

"Cussing in French is still cussing."

I sneered, "You don't even know French."

"I know all the important cuss words in five languages."

Baby tried to lick me in sympathy.

"Stop, Baby. I know you're trying to be kind, but I don't want to have to take a bath right now."

Franklin helped Baby onto the bed, where he could really get at me. He relished licking my face and neck. Oh, well.

"You need to get that dog a ramp or steps, so he can get on the bed."

"I don't want Baby on my bed. He'll ruin the mattress."

"We're getting off point here."

I shook my head wearily. "What is the point?"

"What are you going to do about my brother?"

"I'm not doing anything about your brother," I replied defiantly.

"He's the injured party here."

"So you say."

Franklin fired back, "So he is."

"I'm not so sure."

"I told you what my brother told me."

"Again, so what?"

"Are you implying my brother lies or has bad intentions?"

I shrugged.

"My brother and I have many differences, but Hunter is a man of honor."

I didn't respond.

"You beat all, you know that, Josiah?" Franklin left my bedroom, slamming the door with such force a painting fell off the wall.

Merde!

24

I put the entire unpleasant incident behind me.

I was busy harvesting honey. It took me two days to harvest the honey and another day to extract the honey from the frames.

I hate extracting honey from the honeycomb. It's a messy, sticky business. Plus all the bees smell the honey, and are constantly banging against the windows of the honey house, trying to gain access to honey–their honey.

To get bees away from the honey house, I put the empty frames out in a field for them to clean the honey residue and take it back to the hives. Worked like a charm.

Now the honey was harvested, I needed to strain it, getting out all the bits of combs and other bee debris still in it. Some customers like bee debris left in the honey, thinking it makes the honey more beneficial, but I don't.

I like a clean-looking honey. I don't mind microscopic bits of pollen and beeswax, but I don't like seeing stuff with the naked eye, even though honey never goes bad because of the hydrogen peroxide in it. That's right–hydrogen peroxide. The bees make it.

Aren't honeybees fabulous!

Honey never goes bad, even when it crystallizes. Only Americans insist on eating honey in its liquid form. Other cultures eat honey in its crystallized state, or after it's been whipped into a butter-like paste.

After spending the entire day in the honey house, I made my way back to the Butterfly, wanting nothing more than a hot shower and something to eat.

Low and behold, a red Avanti was in my driveway. Walter Neff was back in town.

I had sent him to Charleston, South Carolina, where Sandy Sloan mentioned she had kinfolk.

Walter must have something to report.

I hurried to the house.

25

Walter was rummaging through my refrigerator with Baby and Georgie sitting patiently beside him, wagging their tails, hoping for a treat.

"Walter, how did you get into the house?"

Without missing a beat, Walter replied, "Picked the lock. You got any mustard to go with this roast beef? I like the spicy brown mustard."

I went into the pantry and retrieved mustard, vinegar, potato chips and Ale-8, a local soft drink, which Walter liked and made a plate for him.

Walter happily slapped his sandwich and dill pickles on the plate. "Put some mustard on my sandwich while I fix my drink, will ya, Toots?"

I dutifully put mustard and mayo on his sandwich while Walter fussed around, putting ice in a glass for his soft drink.

Since he looked tired, I didn't pepper Walter with

questions, but I was aching to know what he had found out in Charleston–if anything.

We both realized it would be a long shot when Walter left, but maybe he had discovered something important.

Leaving Walter in the great room eating with his two canine companions begging for a morsel of his sandwich, I went to shower and change my clothes.

After cleaning myself up, I hurried to talk with Walter only to find him in the guest bedroom sleeping the sleep of the angels, with Baby and Georgie on the bed snoring alongside him. At least he had taken his shoes off before dropping into bed.

Drat!

Resigning myself to waiting, I retrieved Walter's bag from the car and washed his dirty clothes. While he lived with me, I had washed Walter's nasty underwear more times than I cared to remember. Besides, Walter didn't have anything I hadn't seen before, and I always used a disinfectant in the washer afterwards. You can't be too careful with Walter.

After I washed, dried, and folded his clothes, I went out and gave his Avanti a quick wash, knowing my gravel road always threw dust on his prized possession. Besides, I took the opportunity to snoop in his car.

Nothing. Ah, shoot.

Now I was exhausted and dirty again, but I went to bed filthy.

I'd see Walter in the morning.

Good night, y'all.

26

I awoke to the smell of bacon frying and Baby barking—not his warning bark, but the "I want bacon" bark.

Sore from all the hard work I had done the past week, I took a hot shower, trying to work out the kinks in my back while planning my day. I still had to bottle honey and stick labels on the jars.

But first I needed to find out what Walter had discovered.

"Morning," said Walter rather cheerfully. "I made breakfast for us."

"So I see."

"Sit down. Sit down. The eggs are ready."

I sat down while Walter served bacon and scrambled eggs. The table was already set with plates, silverware, orange juice, and butter for the toast.

After serving, Walter joined me and began eating with relish.

I hate to admit it, but the bacon was the way I liked it, and the eggs cooked soft. It was a good meal to start the day, but as I was eating I wondered how long this game of cat and mouse would last. Finally, I blurted, "Dang it, Walter. The suspense is killing me. What did you find out?"

Grinning, Walter leaned over and chucked me under the chin. "You were right to send me to Charleston."

"Walter, I'm gonna stab you with my fork if you don't spill."

"You're always threatening me."

"WALTER!"

Walter stood up and pulled a parcel from behind the couch. He handed it to me.

It was a rectangular package. I looked at him expectantly. "It can't be."

"It is."

I carefully unwrapped the package and studied the contents. It was a small painting of a lovely seascape with two S's at the bottom–Sandy Sloan's signature.

Since I had helped Sandy catalogue all her paintings, I knew this painting had to be recent.

Sandy Sloan was alive!

27

"Did you talk with Sandy?" I asked.

Walter leaned back, looking smug. "No, but I tailed her for a couple of days. The broad didn't have a clue she was being followed. Here's her address." He tossed over a piece of paper with her address and phone.

"Is she living under an assumed name?"

He shook his head. "Mrs. Sloan is using her real name, and walking around as free as you please."

"Tell me about it."

"I first contacted her kinfolk. She has an older half-brother living in the area. He said he didn't know where Sandy was and hadn't seen her for years. I've been in this business a long time. I know when folks are lying. I watched the brother's house, but nothing. So I started hitting all the galleries in the area, and found one that carried her paintings.

"I acted like I really liked her work and wanted to meet the artist. Since I bought the painting, the gallery owner told me she had a little street kiosk near some sweetgrass basket artists on Saturday mornings for several hours during the tourist season.

"I waited till Saturday and went to the location given. From my car, I made an identification from the picture you gave me. I followed her home. She lives in Folly Beach." He pointed to the piece of paper he had given me. "That's her address and phone. Now I've done what you asked. We're even."

I nodded. "Thank you, Walter. If you will give me your receipts, I will write you a check before you leave this morning."

Walter looked crestfallen, but I ignored it. I knew he wanted to stay, but I couldn't have that. Instead, I asked, "Why didn't you talk to her?"

"I'm not going to confront a crazy woman who might have killed her husband. That wasn't part of the deal. You asked me to see if Sandy Sloan was still alive and I did."

"So you know about Toby? They found his body after you left."

"Of course I do. I'm a professional."

"Did you contact the police about Sandy?"

"Not part of the job description. You're going to have to make that call," Walter added.

I was thankful. "I'm glad you didn't call the police. I think I might go see Sandy and see what she has to say. She might not know her house has burned or that Toby is dead."

"Why can't I stay? You have this big, empty house with all these bedrooms, and the dogs love me."

Ignoring Walter's whining, I asked, "Where are your receipts?"

Looking perturbed, Walter answered, "On your desk in a folder."

"If you wait, I'll write you a check now. Thank you for breakfast. You cook up some mean eggs." I rose and went into my study, finding the folder. Quickly calculating the receipts, the total was a little more than expected (I wasn't expecting to purchase a painting), but every item seemed on the up-and-up. I wrote the check and took it to Walter, but he was not in the great room. I checked the guest bedroom. Not there either. I checked outside.

His Avanti was gone.

Walter must have been really upset, since he left without his check. He was all about money.

Oh well, he'd get over it as soon as he cooled down. Walter would eventually see it was impossible for him to live at the Butterfly.

I put the check in an envelope, and put it with the outgoing mail. Then I filed the entire matter in the back of my mind. I had more honey to bottle for my next stint at the Farmer's Market.

I would think about Sandy Sloan and Walter Neff later.

Big mistake.

28

I was weeding my herb garden when I heard a rustling. Looking up, I saw Hunter meandering through the dirt pathway toward me.

"Hello."

"Hello," I replied, taking off my gloves.

"Got a moment?"

"Sure."

"Let's sit on the bench."

Hunter took my basket and laid it aside as we sat down. "I want to apologize for the other day. At the time, I didn't understand why you had such a visceral reaction to seeing Ellen."

"You're on a first-name basis with her?"

"What should I call her?"

"Witch would be a good word, if you began it with the letter b."

Hunter grinned. "I really didn't know about the

history between the two of you. If I had known, I never would have agreed to meet with her before our date."

"Thank you for the apology. I'm sorry too. I overreacted. I don't know what happened. As soon as I saw her sitting with you, I lost my breath and my heart started pounding."

"It was a panic attack."

"You think so?"

Hunter nodded as he put his hand over mine.

I didn't pull away.

"It was a full-blown attack."

I didn't reply, because I needed to think about what Hunter said. The mere sight of Ellen should not have caused such an extreme reaction. I had behaved childishly.

Hunter continued, "Franklin filled me in on what happened between you and your late husband, Brannon. It sounded like a pretty nasty state of affairs."

"Brannon's behavior was perfectly awful."

"And you blame Ellen for it?"

"Yes and no. I'm sure she egged him on, but Brannon never did anything he didn't want to do. He wanted to hurt me a great deal after he left—and he did.

"Did you ever find out why?"

"I tracked Brannon to Keeneland one day and confronted him. The only thing he would tell me was that he didn't love me anymore, in fact, he hated me."

"That must have been hurtful to discover."

"I didn't feel anything for days. I guess I was in shock or denial, but later, when I bounced back, I made the divorce brutal for him. Ellen claims the stress of the divorce proceedings ruined his health and caused his heart attack. She may be right."

"So the divorce was never finalized?"

"No, I'm officially a widow, but I could never find our liquid assets. He hid them very well. I guess Ellen is enjoying the money I earned from thirty years of hard work. Brannon cleaned out our joint accounts and sold off our stock options before he left."

Inwardly, I winced. The entire mess of my divorce was embarrassing, so why was I telling Hunter? I decided to be more positive. "That's old history. I didn't have it as bad as some women who were cheated in a divorce. I had the farm, my bees, my daughter, and good friends who helped me through.

"I now see how I was played by her."

"I thought you knew about us."

"The only thing Franklin told me was that you were a widow."

"That's all?"

"That's all."

"I've never known Franklin to be so discreet."

Hunter chuckled. "Frightening, isn't it?" He gave my hand a little squeeze. "I want to tell you something else."

I looked expectantly at him.

"I didn't buy a horse from Ellen's stable. I bought a horse from another farm."

I breathed a sigh of relief. "Thank you for that."

"Which brings me to ask a favor of you. I don't have time at the moment to take care of the horse. I was wondering if you have room to board her until the stables at Wickliffe Manor are repaired."

"I think so."

"That's settled. I'll bring her over in the next couple of days."

"No problem. I'm glad we set things right. Acrimony between us didn't sit right with me."

"I have one more piece of jam to put on your bread."

Not liking the serious look on Hunter's face, I braced myself.

"I was at the police station this morning and overheard several officers talking. It seems someone tipped them off that Sandy Sloan is alive and living in South Carolina's low country. They're bringing her back as a person of interest in Toby Sloan's death and the arson of their house."

"So Toby didn't commit suicide."

"It appears not. Toby was shot by a shotgun on the left side of the face with the driver's window three-fourths up. There was no way he could have maneuvered that type of big gun with the window closed. The police think he was shot with the window open and then the killer closed it, leaving enough space at the top to allow the truck to fill with water and sink when it went into the river. The killer kept the gun when he left the scene."

"Do you think Sandy did it?" I asked.

"She is their number-one suspect in her husband's death. I say, oh boy, watch out."

I turned my face away from Hunter, afraid my expression might betray my complicity concerning Sandy.

Oh Walter, Walter. What have you done?

29

Three days later, I was sitting across from Sandy Sloan in the Fayette County Detention Center, which was built to look like a horse barn.

"Josiah, it's so good to see a friendly face," said Sandy, looking haggard.

"Did Shaneika Mary Todd come to see you?" I asked.

"Yes, this morning. Thank you for recommending her."

"Are you going to retain her?"

Sandy pursed her lips for a moment and then sucked on a finger before speaking. "It looks like I'll have to. Ms. Todd said they might charge me for arson. I don't see why. The house wasn't insured." Tears pooled in Sandy's eyes.

"You set the house on fire?"

"Ms. Todd said I'm not supposed to talk about it."

"Have the police talked to you about Toby?"

She began to cry. "Josiah, I didn't hurt Toby. I didn't even know he was dead. I swear it on the Bible." She heaved big sobs of misery. Tears fell at a copious rate and stained her inmate uniform.

A guard warned that if she didn't control herself, Sandy would have to go back to her cell.

"Can I give her a handkerchief?" I asked the guard. He nodded yes.

Reaching into my purse, I pulled out a hanky and gave it to Sandy while the guard watched closely.

"Pull yourself together, or they're going to make me leave."

Sandy blew her nose twice.

The guard made her give the hanky back, so I put the nasty, wet thing in my pocket.

"Sandy, I don't have much time," I said, glancing at the guard.

Sandy also glanced at the guard while leaning toward me.

The guard slapped his nightstick against the wall in a warning. "No touching."

We both sat up straight in our chairs.

"How's Georgie? You still have her?"

Smiling, I nodded. "She's fine, Sandy. I'll keep her until you get out of this place. Georgie has missed you terribly."

"I wanted to take her with me, but how could I? I was afraid she'd get hurt somehow."

"So you *did* set the house on fire?"

Sandy avoided eye contact by looking down at the table. "Josiah, did the police find Toby's watch? It was my father's old Omega Seamaster watch, and he set great store by it. I'd like to have it back."

"I don't know if they found his watch, Sandy. Other things are more important than your father's watch at the moment. I think you should concentrate on how you're going to answer the police when they come calling. They will want to know why you would set the house on fire with your paintings and cash inside, and then why your husband shows up dead."

"If I did–and I'm not saying that I did–it was because I had to leave Toby, you see. I had made my mind up months previously that I was going to leave him. I found out he had been adulterating my medication, trying to make me look crazy."

My expression must have been one of disbelief because Sandy drew back hastily.

"I can see you don't believe me, Josiah, but it's true. He was taking my capsules and replacing the medication with cornstarch. I had them analyzed."

"I believe you, Sandy. I realize people do fantastic things, but why would Toby do such a thing? What did he have to gain by it?"

Sandy looked around to see if anyone was listening. "He had found a new cutie and wanted to run with her."

"How did you find out?"

"She called me, big as brass, and told me she and Toby were in love. Said they wanted to get married, and I was in the way."

"Did you get her name?"

"It was Carol Elliott. She lives in Winchester."

"Did you confront Toby?"

"Yes, I did. He said they had seen each other, but he had dropped her. She wouldn't let go, and was stirring up trouble to get back at him."

"Did you believe Toby?"

"No. I followed him one day to her house and peeked in the window. They were very lovey dovey. Toby lied to me. That's when I decided to divorce him."

"Many men play around, but they don't always leave their wives. It sounds like she was getting desperate. Maybe Toby had no intention of leaving you, but that doesn't explain the problem with your medication."

"My paintings had started to command a pretty sum. With a divorce, he would no longer have access to my paintings or my talent, but with me declared mentally incompetent, he could still control my money and my entire collection."

"That's why you emptied your savings account and left your paintings in the fire?"

"I threw his half of the money in the fire. I kept my half and went to live near my kin to start a new life. As for my paintings, I could paint more." Sandy tapped on the table. "Toby was going to get what was coming to him. I meant to leave him destitute."

"Let's say you were at your house when the fire started. What happened then?"

"I picked up my bag and left. As far as I was concerned, I had symbolically killed my old life. That's all it was supposed to be. No one was to be hurt. Toby must have come home, and thinking I had perished in the fire, felt regret and committed suicide. That's the only explanation."

"Sandy, didn't the police tell you?"

"Tell me what? I haven't talked to them yet."

"The coroner determined Toby didn't commit suicide. His death was murder. He was shot to death by a shotgun and thrown into the river."

Sandy's hand flew up to her mouth. Her neck and face grew red.

"Sandy?"

She stood up, causing her chair to fall backwards. With a look of horror on her face, Sandy ran from the visitor's room.

The guard righted the chair. "You better go," he said.

Astonished, I gathered my purse and left.

The guard seemed relieved to see me leave.

Not as relieved as I was to be leaving.

30

"Sandy has ruined her life," I said.

"Maybe. Sandy certainly set events in motion when she torched her house, it would seem," admonished Shaneika.

I replied, "That's a little harsh. You act like you don't believe her. Why are you representing Sandy, if you don't believe her innocence?"

Shaneika shrugged. She was wearing the beige Chanel suit with black piping–my favorite suit of hers. And she had a new 'do. It was her natural black color, shaved almost down to the skull–just a little stubble. The short haircut made her hazel eyes seem larger. She looked both fierce and sophisticated.

"Did she confess to anything?" asked Shaneika.

"She talked around starting the fire, but said she did not kill Toby."

"And your thoughts?"

"Sandy didn't make sense. She said she thought Toby

assumed she had died in the fire. Feeling deep regret, he killed himself. She became upset when I told her Toby hadn't committed suicide, but was murdered. What difference did it matter how he died? Dead is dead," I said.

"I don't understand this suicide angle myself. Why would Toby think she died in the fire when Sandy left her clothes at the cliffside, hoping people would think she jumped off."

"Exactly. Let's say Toby does think Sandy is dead, and now realizes he really loved her and wants to commit suicide. Why wouldn't he shoot himself or jump off the cliff there? Why would he travel miles to drive his truck into the river at Winchester and then shoot himself as the truck is sinking? There are too many holes in the tale Sandy told me. I think she's holding back. She knows something she's not telling."

Shaneika said, "I don't want you to see her anymore, Josiah."

"Oh," was all I could muster.

Shaneika seemed unmoved. "If you want to help your friend, I need to know everything you know. Okay?"

I nodded while looking for some tissues. I was becoming weepy. The entire affair was hammering my nerves. I couldn't process all the negatives fast enough.

Jumping Jehosaphat! Was I having a nervous breakdown?

Shaneika passed a tissue box over the desk from which I plucked a few tissues to wipe several tears running down my face. She drew in a harsh breath. "Are you all right? I've never seen you this emotional."

"I feel a little overwhelmed at the moment."

"You need to take a rest."

"My leg is bothering me," I replied. It was the staple answer I gave when I didn't wish to discuss an issue.

Shaneika gave me a sympathetic look. "I'll try to hurry."

I nodded. "That would be nice."

"Did you report Sandy's whereabouts to the police?"

"Is this conversation privileged?"

"Yes."

"Walter Neff did. I hired him to find Sandy, which he did. He ratted her out of anger. He was mad because I wouldn't let him live at the Butterfly anymore."

Shaneika shot me a strange look. "Are you and Walter a thing?"

"I wish people wouldn't ask if I'm seeing Walter. It makes me feel queasy."

"Answer the question."

"NO! I think he is still discombobulated over Bunny Witt's death. He hasn't found solid ground yet."

"What a nasty little man. After all you've done for him, you think he'd be a little more grateful."

"You'd think that, wouldn't you?"

"That explains how the police found Sandy. I hope Mr. Neff keeps his mouth shut about that. Now, I want you to tell me everything she said to you at the jail."

I might not remember what I had for breakfast, but I can recall conversations word for word. I told Shaneika almost verbatim what Sandy related to me, while she took notes.

"Let me stop you there and backtrack on something," Shaneika remarked. She pulled out a police report from another file and handed it to me.

It was the police report about Toby claiming Sandy had attacked him with a knife. It contained my statements to the police as well.

"Is the police report correct?"

"Yes."

"Did you believe Toby was telling the truth?"

"I don't know. I've never known Sandy to be violent, but she came close today to admitting she set her house on fire. I don't know what to believe."

"Look down at the bottom."

I glanced down on the report. At the bottom was scrawled JDLR. That was police code for "just doesn't look right." The officer, making the report, was letting others in the police department know there was something hinky about the information.

"I'll have to talk to the reporting officer, but it looks like he didn't believe Toby."

I ruminated, "If Toby was lying, it would fit the story Sandy tells that he was setting her up to look crazy." I leaned over the desk. "I'm curious. Did the DA send over Hunter's report?"

"Yes."

"What did it say?"

"I can't discuss it with you. It's confidential."

"If the DA sent Hunter's report to you, sounds like they are going to charge Sandy with arson."

"They already have."

"Oh, I guess I'll hear the report in court then."

"I doubt it."

"Why?"

"Because the DA plans to call you as a witness."

31

You could have knocked me over with a feather. "Me? Testify for the DA? I won't do it. I won't."

"You can be declared a hostile witness and I can certainly object, but if you don't show up, you will be in contempt of court and thrown in jail."

"Jumping Jehosaphats."

"That's why I don't want you to have any more contact with Sandy Sloan, and keep what she said to yourself. No talking to Franklin."

"Does that mean the DA, too?"

Shaneika's expression hardened. "No, you have to talk to them and tell the truth."

"Just wanted to be sure."

"What's the matter with you? You're usually sharper than this."

"I don't know. I feel confused about this entire matter."

"I'll sort it out. I'll give Sandy Sloan the best defense possible."

"Do you think she killed Toby?"

"She may have, but if she did, I think it was under duress. Sandy might not have been in her right mind. I can tell you the DA is going to stress Sandy had motive and opportunity, but they haven't charged her with murder yet."

"What about Darius Combs or Carol Elliott?"

"I'm looking into it. They also had motive, but did they have opportunity?"

"What kind of gun was Toby killed with?"

"A 12-gauge shotgun."

"Darius Combs pulled a 12-gauge shotgun on me."

"I'm going to pull him into court to present reasonable doubt to the jury. It would have been better if you had reported the incident to the police."

"Darius hated Toby. He might have hated Toby enough to kill him. Why don't the police do a ballistics test on his gun?"

"Because they feel they have their woman. No need." Shaneika tapped a pencil on her desk. "Did the Sloans have a shotgun?"

"An old one. I don't even think it worked. Did they find it in the fire?"

"No. It's probably at the bottom of the Kentucky River." Shaneika looked at her watch. "I have another appointment in a few moments. I need to wind this up."

I stood. "Thanks, girlfriend."

"Go through there," she said, pointing to a door that led directly into the hallway. "And Josiah, remember. No gossiping, especially to Franklin or Lady Elsmere."

I nodded, tucked my tail between my legs and left, wondering how much more damage could I do by trying to be "friend."

32

I meant to call Hunter, but he beat me to the punch by showing up at the stables with his new horse. One of the stable hands called me, saying there was a problem.

I arrived moments later with Baby and Georgie in tow, just in time to see Hunter release a Hanoverian mare into the paddock.

Standing beside Hunter, I watched the horse prance about. "She's a beauty," I said of the dapple-gray horse.

"I was lucky to get her."

"What are you going to do with her?"

"Pleasure riding. I'm too old to compete anymore."

"Hunter, I was planning to call you. I think we may have a problem with you boarding horses with me."

Hunter studied me with those brown eyes of his, making my knees quake a little. I've only seen a look like that twice. It was how Robert Donat looked at

Madeleine Carrol in *The 39 Steps,* and Burt Lancaster at Yvonne De Carlo before they were killed in *Criss Cross.* I don't know how to explain the "look" but it's a mixture of tenderness, amusement, and sadness. Now Hunter had the look. The "look" always got my attention.

"What is it?"

"Um, I can't think of it. Give me a moment." I was completely rattled. I suddenly realized why I had such a negative reaction when I saw Hunter with Ellen.

I WAS JEALOUS!

I hated Ellen for being with Hunter. And I hated Hunter for being with her.

What did Lady Elsmere say–the heart wants what the heart wants, whether it made sense or not.

NO! NO! This can't be happening at my age. I don't want it.

"Josiah?"

I came out of my fog. "I was going to call you to say I don't think it's a good idea to board your horse here."

Hunter gave me the "look" again.

I just about peed in my pants.

"Why not?"

"It seems I am going to have to testify for the DA regarding Sandy Sloan, but I intend to be a hostile witness. Since you were hired by the Fire Department to do a report on the fire, it might be seen as a conflict of interest with you boarding a horse on my property."

"I've taken care of that. I have completely recused myself in the case and returned my fee. They are to have a new forensic psychiatrist make another report."

"Oh."

"Oh? You look disappointed. I thought I cleared up the nonsense with Ellen Boudreaux."

"You did. You did."

"Then what's the problem?"

"It's just that I think . . ."

Hunter cut in, "That's the problem, Josiah. You think too much. You don't trust men, and do everything to push away any man who's interested in you. You also have low self-esteem issues because of your limp."

"Don't forget the hearing aid," I added sardonically.

"That's another thing, I'm tired of your constant sarcasm. You're positively feral at times."

"Is there anything you do like about me? If I'm so blighted, why bother? Just go the other way, sir."

"You're incorrigible, you know that?"

"Blah, blah, blah."

"Shut up. Shut your wicked mouth."

"Make me, big man," I replied defiantly.

"All right, I will." Hunter grabbed me, pulling me close. He tilted my face up and kissed me.

It was a rather long and passionate kiss.

I struggled, let me tell you. I struggled for about two seconds before I melted and pressed against him. Just like in the movies where the woman is unsure, but succumbs to the masculine virility bearing down on her. Oh dear, that sounds filthy, doesn't it—but exciting when it happens—if it happens with a man to whom you are attracted.

Hunter felt strong and muscular. In other words, he felt darn nice.

We kissed a long time. We broke for air, sucked in some oxygen, and then kissed some more.

Hunter pushed me against the fence and really started putting on the dog. My forehead, my neck, my cheeks, my lips. He even kissed and stroked my hair.

Finally, Hunter pulled away and looked at me intently. "Hello, Sugarlips."

"Hello," I answered, kinda goofy, as I was somewhat dazed.

"I'd like to see where this might lead."

"I don't know, Hunter."

"Say yes, you creature."

"I never knew anyone calling me a creature would sound so divine."

"I'm sure the feeling will wear off as soon as you have time to think about it. Look, I know my having two past wives gives you pause. It was never because I beat them or didn't share my wealth. It was because of my mistress–work. I neglected them, so they found other chaps who were home more often. But I'm slowing down now, and can take the time to be a real companion to a woman who might appreciate what I have to offer.

"Josiah, I want a good life, a quality life. I think I can make that happen in the Bluegrass. I've come home to stay. I would like to see more of you on a regular basis–if you will let me."

"I'm afraid of being hurt."

"So am I."

"You being hurt by me?"

"Ain't that a kicker? I'm surprised myself."

"You sound like Mr. Darcy proposing to Elizabeth Bennet."

"Who?"

"Mr. Darcy."

"I'm not proposing marriage."

"I didn't say you were. I'm saying you're insulting me like Mr. Darcy when he proposed to Elizabeth Bennet in *Pride and Prejudice*."

"Can we have at least one conversation which does not include a reference to a movie, book, or play?"

"Have you read it?"

"*Pride and Prejudice*? Yes, I have. Can we get back on track? You're trying to divert the issue I wish to discuss."

"No, I'm not."

"I realize you're afraid. Please consider my gift of friendship."

I was still hesitant.

Hunter sensing this, suggested, "Let's do this. We'll take it one day at a time, no strings attached. If either one of us wants to end the relationship, he or she can call it off–no questions asked."

I felt comfortable with Hunter's thinking. Nothing permanent–a friendship that could easily be dissolved–a way out if things got too sticky. I always needed a back door escape where men were concerned. "I can do that. Nothing too fast, though."

"No gentleman would insist on more than the lady can handle."

"Let's shake on it," I said.

"Let's kiss on it," Hunter suggested, gathering me close.

"Excuse me. So sorry, but excuse me."

We both looked over to see a man staring at us, smirking. "Gotta get the trailer back, Mac."

Hunter let go of me so quickly, I stumbled. So much for chivalry.

"Yes, you can let her out." Hunter said to the man.

"Okay, Mac." The man tipped his hat at me. "Ma'am."

"What's he talking about, Hunter?"

"Something else I bought. Wait."

The man led a small piebald horse out of the trailer.

I looked at Hunter. "You bought another horse?"

"What do you think of her?"

"She's a beautiful horse. Very unusual markings. A black medicine hat and shield on her chest." (A medicine hat is the color on a horse's ears and poll with the rest of the face a different color. The marking looks similar to a hat on the horse's head. A shield refers to a block of color on the horse's chest.)

The man stopped in front of us, giving me a good look at the horse. She was a small black and white American Paint horse."

"Is she a pony?"

"She's not considered a pony, although she's small for her breed."

"Hunter, she has blue eyes."

Hunter stepped forward and looked. "She sure does. Not as pretty as your green eyes, though."

The Paint stepped forward and nuzzled my shoulder. I scratched her ears, enjoying the earthy scent all horses have.

"She cottons to you, Josiah."

"She does seem to like me."

"That's good, because she's for you."

I jumped back. "Me! What am I going to do with a horse?"

"Ride her."

"I can't ride." I slapped my leg.

"Yes, you can."

"I can't afford a horse. Horses are expensive. I should know, since I charge an arm and a leg to board them here."

Hunter signaled to the man he could go, and took the piebald's reins.

"She's legally mine, but I want you to ride her."

"No can do. I might fall. I'm held together with spit and wire as it is. I don't need a broken hip as well."

"She has nowhere else to go. She's a middle-aged horse no one wants, but there are still some good years in her. I want you to see something. Look under there," he said, pointing to the mare's belly.

I bent down as much as I could. The horse turned her head, nipping at my buttocks. I patted her side to comfort her. "I'm not going to hurt you, old gal. Just want a look-see."

I felt along her abdomen. Straightening up, I leaned against the horse's side. "I feel scars."

"Best I can tell, someone used spurs on her."

"A lot, I would say." I wondered who rode with spurs anymore.

Hunter remained silent, watching me gently stroke the Paint.

"She sure is pretty," I mused.

"She sure as shootin' is."

"Are you turning into Hop-a-long Cassidy on me? Next you'll be saying 'aw shucks ma'am, t'warn't nothing',' and rolling your own cigarettes."

"I'm trying to create a certain mood here. Just go with it."

"And you say she's got nowhere to stay?"

"She's the companion horse to my Hanoverian. The owner said if I didn't take her, he was going to shoot her, since no one would want such an old horse."

"How old is she?"

"Fourteen."

"That's not old for a horse. They can live to be thirty."

"About your age in horse years, wouldn't you say?"

I ignored Hunter's last remark. "Of course, she can stay, but I don't believe you about the owner shooting her. She would make a good riding pony for a young person. As for me riding, that's absurd. I was never a good rider when I was young, and now an English saddle is out of the question."

"This mare is not an English saddle kind of horse. A western saddle is for her. You can ride western-style. The horn will help steady you."

"I don't know."

Hunter led the Paint into the paddock with his majestic Hanoverian before taking her off the lead. The Paint slowly followed as the other horse went to the water trough. Together they stretched their necks to drink.

"They seem to enjoy each other's company," I admitted.

Hunter looked at his watch. "I'm late. Meeting a contractor about the house."

"Don't worry about your horses. I'll check on them every day. We'll take good care of your babies."

"Think about what I said." Hunter took a long look at his horses before taking off.

Hunter's kisses were all I could think about the rest of the day, but I had to bottle honey.

Before dark, I went back to the horse barn and checked on the horses. They had settled in nicely. Tomorrow I would tell the stable hand to let them out in the front pasture.

To my way of thinking, my saying no to riding was the end of the discussion about me getting up on a horse, so I wasn't thrilled when a Spanish saddle with silver buckles arrived at the Butterfly special delivery the next day. I would have to say it had the biggest horn on a saddle I had ever seen.

It seemed Hunter was determined that I ride.
We'll see who wins that battle.

33

I didn't see Hunter for the next few weeks. He was busy with refurbishing his house and out of town on business.

I kept an eye on his horses. Several times a week I would go to the stable to brush the Paint. When she saw me standing at the fence, she always wandered over. It might have been the cubes of sugar I had in my pocket that caused her to be so compliant, or maybe it was my company. I'm sure that's wishful thinking, but I enjoyed brushing the mare while telling her my troubles. She would nod her head as though agreeing.

I could tell the Hanoverian and the American Paint were gaining weight, which pleased me to no end. I thought they had looked a little thin when they first arrived.

Every so often, Hunter would call. We would talk about his horses. He was interested to hear that the

Hanoverian had a fondness for apples while the pony liked sugar. The subjects for conversation centered around them and his house. He never brought up our relationship, or when we would see each other again.

I took this as a sign he was having second thoughts about us, so I left it alone. We had made a deal, hadn't we? No questions asked.

I was resolved to be a good sport about it. After all, it had only been a few kisses. Nothing serious.

So why did I keep thinking about him?

Determined to push Hunter from my mind, I concentrated on Sandy's situation. I felt bad for her. Real bad. I wanted to help her, but how? And if she really murdered Toby, should I be wasting my time?

Since her bail was high, she was still in jail. Shaneika couldn't shake the judge on the amount. The only positive thing in Sandy's life was her paintings, which were commanding record prices, but the galleries were slow to deposit Sandy's share of the sales in her new bank account.

Shaneika issued stern letters that Sandy was entitled to her percentage, and would sue if the money was not deposited immediately, but so far—nothing.

I took a few photos of Georgie, which Shaneika took to Sandy. Shaneika told me the photos of Georgie brought Sandy some peace, but she was still under medical care and losing weight. Shaneika wanted to get her out on bail.

I felt useless. Eunice had our business running shipshape. I had bottled all my honey. The farm was humming along with the help of Charles Dupuy's grandsons. There was nothing for me to do until Saturday when I would be at the Farmer's Market.

Boredom is a rotten thing. It can lead to all sorts of mischief. What's that old saying about idle hands being the devil's workshop—and how did it affect me?

This way—I called Shaneika. Had she talked to Carol Elliott, Toby's girlfriend?

"No."

"Why not?" I asked.

"Because we can't locate Carol Elliott."

"You don't find that odd?"

"I do, but the police don't."

"I would think the police would want to talk to her, since Toby's body was found near Winchester, and Carol Elliott lives in Winchester."

"You would think," Shaneika responded with her signature sarcasm.

"Has Sandy been charged with Toby's murder?"

"Not yet."

"That means they don't have enough evidence."

"I concur."

"Hmm. You know, Shaneika, I'm not doing anything special today."

"It's a nice day for a drive."

"That's what I was thinking. Maybe a little jaunt over to Winchester."

"If you get caught, I will have to disavow any knowledge of your actions."

"Will this tape self-destruct in five seconds?"

"What tape?"

"Shaneika, it's hard to be witty with you when you don't even recognize pop culture references. Disavow any knowledge of your actions. Tape will self-destruct in five seconds. Hellooo. *Mission Impossible.*"

Ignoring my banter, Shaneika mumbled Carol Elliott's address before cutting me off.

I was still explaining *Mission Impossible* when I noticed the line was dead. I was talking to thin air. No matter. I had something to sink my teeth into.

I let the dogs out to do their business before putting them back in the house. Each dog, sucking on a chew toy, settled in nicely for a nap. "I'll only be gone for a couple of hours," I said to them.

Baby already had his eyes closed, gumming his toy like a pacifier. Georgie rose and followed me to the door, wagging her tail, assuming she'd be riding shotgun with me.

"No, Georgie, I can't take you this time. You stay here and be good. We'll go for a walk when I get back."

Leaving Georgie to her own devices, I locked the front door and hurried to my car. Driving the back roads, it took only a short time to reach Winchester. I wasn't sure where Mrs. Elliott's street was located, so I pulled over and consulted a map. Yes—a real honest-to-goodness paper map.

It took me a few seconds to find her street, and make the connection where I was. I pulled out again, turned left, went several streets down, and turned right again.

Carol Elliott's house was at the end of a cul-de-sac. It was a modest, white clapboard house, neatly kept, with woods framing the backyard and the left side of the house. There was a sedan in the driveway.

I knocked on the front door still thinking about what I was going to say. I briefly considered telling the truth. I knocked again and rang the doorbell.

Nobody answered.

I went around to the back and knocked on the back door. Nobody. I peered in the window. The lights were off, and the house seemed empty.

"He's not home."

I swirled around, grateful I was wearing a blond wig, even though it looked dreadful. "What?"

A woman was standing in the yard next door, hanging up her laundry to dry. "Lonny's not home. He's at work." She pulled some clothespins out of her pocket and hung up a pair of pants.

"I'm here to see Carol. Isn't that her car?" I was making a guess. It was a Toyota Corolla, a car a woman would drive.

The neighbor glanced at the car. Her expression was odd. Maybe curiosity. Maybe concern. I couldn't quite interpret it.

"Yeah. That's her car, but she's not home." She began hanging up cloth diapers.

"Carol loaned me some money, and I came to pay it back." So much for the truth.

"Try the back door."

"This door?" I asked, pointing.

"Yeah, nobody in this neighborhood locks their back door."

"Isn't that unsafe?"

"Nah, nothing bad ever happens on our street. We all look out for one another."

"Oh," I replied. "Do they have any mean dogs?"

Shaking her head, the woman went about hanging up her clothes, most of them baby clothes. She obviously had a newborn.

I tried the doorknob.

It turned.

I quietly opened the door and stuck my head in the kitchen. "Hello," I called. "Hello."

Silence.

I stepped inside. "Hello, Carol. Are you home?"

Nothing.

"I'm in the kitchen. Please don't shoot me, anyone. Hello?"

Silence greeted me. The house was dark and gloomy.

Sensing that no one was really in the house, I grew bolder, taking the opportunity to snoop. I put on gloves I had in my pocket, and wiped off the doorknob. One can't be too careful was how I looked at it. Now I had to be quick.

I went through the mail on the kitchen table. Just bills. Then I ventured into the hall, glancing in the living room. It was neat. Very neat. Carol must be a clean freak.

After calling out again and hearing no response, I found the bathroom, and opened the medicine cabinet.

There were women's toiletries like hairspray and moisturizer in the cabinet. Also a bottle of Prozac. It was prescribed for Carol and was almost full. I looked at the date on the bottle. Dated several weeks before Toby died. I put it back. Before I left, I checked the blond wig in the mirror. It looked absolutely hideous on me, but it was on straight. That's all that mattered.

Next I went to find Carol's bedroom. Down the hall, I found two bedrooms, again both tidy. I chose the bigger one. The bed was made, and the floor free of discarded clothes or shoes.

There was a hamper in the corner. I went through it. Nothing but men's clothes.

I checked the closet. It was stuffed full of both women's and men's clothing, purses, shoe boxes, and mismatched luggage.

I had to speed this up.

Glancing around the room, I noticed a jewelry box on the dresser. I hurried over and rummaged through it. Underneath some costume jewelry was a band of gold. A woman's wedding ring. I looked for an inscription. There was none, but the band was heavily scratched. I put it back, closing the box.

On the dresser were perfume and a hairbrush. On instinct, I pulled some hair out of the brush and put it in a ziplock sandwich bag from my pocket. Now I had to get out. Carol or her husband could come home any moment.

I went next door and knocked.

The neighbor came to the door.

"Sorry to bother you again, but I left the money on the table. If you see her, tell her to look for it under the salt and pepper shakers. I don't want her to miss it."

"I don't know when that will be."

"But her car is in the driveway."

"Yes, but I haven't seen her several months now, and the car hasn't been moved."

"Several months? That's why I could never get ahold of her. Do you know where she went?"

The neighbor glanced over at the house, again with a strange look on her face. "Lonny said Carol ran off with some man."

"And left her car?"

A shrug of her shoulder was her only reply.

I tried another tactic. "I found her wedding ring on the floor. I put it back up on the table."

"Was it cut?"

"No. It was intact."

"Carol gained some weight and couldn't get it off. She was going to have it cut off by a jeweler."

I could tell the woman was getting antsy. I had to hurry with my questions. "I noticed all the curtains and blinds were closed. I've never known Carol to do that. It makes the house so dark."

"That didn't start until Carol left."

"I see Lonny is starting a garden. The earth is turned over near the back of the yard."

"I'm busy. I need to go." The woman shut the door in my face.

I went to my car, noticing the neighbor was peeking out from behind a drape. Oh, great. I hoped she didn't take down my license plate number. And I hoped she didn't tell Lonny Elliott about my visit, though I had a strong hunch she avoided Lonny Elliott like the plague. Like me, the neighbor knew something was not right in the house of Elliott.

34

"The police searched the river thoroughly. Carol Elliott is not in the Kentucky River where Toby was found," said Shaneika, sitting behind her massive desk.

"Then where is she?" I asked.

"She could be anywhere, Jo. The problem is, there is no evidence to support any theory you might concoct. Let's say Carol Elliott killed Toby in a jealous rage because he wouldn't leave Sandy. Here's another one– Sandy killed them both in a jealous rage. Interesting theories, but nothing to back them up.

"Listen, Josiah, maybe she realized nothing could ever come of her affair with Toby. She grew despondent and left town. You said you saw a prescription for depression."

"And leave her car behind? Her medication? Her clothes?"

"Perhaps she used a friend's car or a rental. Perhaps, like Sandy, Carol Elliott was symbolically putting an end to her old life, and that included clothes and her car."

"Her wedding ring? Her neighbor said she couldn't get it off her finger. It was too tight."

"You don't know it was her wedding ring you saw. It could have been her mother's."

"Come on, Shaneika. Have a little more imagination."

"I deal in facts."

"Lawyers deal in facts? They deal in perceptions. In what they can make a jury believe."

"I'll ignore your sarcasm." She stared hard at me. I stared back.

"Okay. I'll talk with the lead detective on Toby's murder case, and encourage him to talk to Lonny Elliott, but I'm not promising anything will come out of it."

"That's fair."

"By the way, did you happen to find a shotgun in their house?" Shaneika asked.

"No, but I didn't have time to search the entire house. I didn't see a computer either, but I do have this." I pulled a wad of hair out of my pocket and placed it on Shaneika's desk.

"Good lord, what is that?"

"I think it's Carol Elliott's hair."

"What am I supposed to do with it?"

"Keep it. Might come in useful for DNA testing."

"Evidence has to be collected and handled properly. This hair is inadmissible."

"Just hang on to it. You never know."

Shaneika reached into a drawer and took out a large manila envelope, sliding the plastic bag with the hair into it. After sealing the envelope, she notated date and time on it. "I'll lock it up in my safe, but we won't ever be able to use it."

"Like I said, you never know," I replied before taking my leave. "You never know."

35

Weeks passed slowly. I didn't hear from Shaneika, and even though I was desperate to hear the outcome of Shaneika's talk with the police, I was resigned to wait—not my favorite thing, but sometimes these things take time.

A knock sounded on the door. I looked at the camera monitor.

It was Hunter!

I opened the door and Hunter rushed in. Grabbing me, he bent me over, cradling my head and gave me a long, passionate kiss. I meant to complain about his hot and cold nature with me, but somewhere along the kiss, I forgot.

"Been thinking about this kiss for a long time."

"Could have fooled me," I replied. "The phone calls have been quite platonic."

"We're too old for phone sex."

"Are we?"

Hunter winked. "Is that an invitation?"

I stepped away from him. "Cool down. I hardly know you."

"I knew you'd be that way, so why bother on the phone. You'd just hang up."

"There are proper ways to do things. I haven't received the mandatory flowers or candy yet."

Hunter rubbed his chin. "Ah, the traditional accoutrements of courtship. You really are old school."

"So are you. Don't deny it."

"Mea culpa. It's true." Hunter looked around. "Anyone here?"

I shook my head.

"Offer me a drink, and tell all about yourself since I've been away."

"Where did you go?"

"Seattle to work on a case, and I have a nice big check in my pocket, a good chunk of which I plan to spend on you."

"I like the sound of that."

"Drink first, then talk. We need to catch up."

I made a Mint Julep for him, complete with crushed ice from the walk-in freezer and a sprig of mint from my back terrace. I had club soda, determined to cut down on my drinking. We sat on my long mid-century couch in the great room, and we talked, or rather, I talked–even telling him about going to Carol Elliott's house, and how I was on pins and needles, waiting to see if Shaneika talked to the police about her.

Hunter nodded occasionally, and sipped his bourbon drink every now and then. When I ran out of wind, he said, "Do you always take chances like that? I mean Carol Elliott could have been sleeping in her bed, or Lonny Elliott could have been taking a walk in the woods and come home."

"But they weren't. Please don't scold. I lost my taste for men telling me what to do a long time ago."

"I see." He put his drink down and put his arm around me. "Was that all of it?"

"I think so."

"I'm so glad you confided in me. I know it was hard for you."

I nodded.

Hunter pulled me closer. "We will have to celebrate this momentous occasion. Shall we go out to dinner tonight?" He looked at his watch. "I have enough time to go to the bank, cash this check, and come back for you."

I started to suggest a restaurant when the doorbell rang. "I wonder who that could be?" I said, rising.

Looking into the camera monitor, I couldn't believe it. I threw open the door.

Standing before me was Sandy Sloan!

36

"Sandy! My goodness! Come in. Come in."

Sandy stood rooted at the door, looking somewhat sour. "I'd rather not. I've come for Georgie. Is she still here?" Her voice sounded harsh.

Confused at Sandy's unfriendliness, I answered, "Yes, I'll call her."

"Don't bother. I'll call for her. GEORGIE! GEORGIE!"

Both dogs ran into the great room, looked around and, seeing me in the foyer, raced to the front door.

It only took Georgie seconds to recognize Sandy. She scampered to Sandy, jumping up and down at her owner's feet, filled with joy.

Sandy picked her up and abruptly began walking away.

"Just a minute, Sandy. Isn't there something you want to say to me?"

Sandy turned around.

Her expression was so full of malevolence, I stepped back.

Sensing something was not right, Baby stood between us, looking back and forth. I could tell he was confused by the perturbed tone of my voice. I gave him a reassuring pat.

"I've taken care of Georgie for months. I don't expect any type of reimbursement, but a simple thank-you would be nice."

"Should I also thank you for getting me thrown in jail? Should I thank you for telling the police where I was? You always have to butt in other folk's business, don't you, Josiah?"

I was dumbfounded. "Sandy, that wasn't my fault. The police were looking for you after they found Toby. It would only have been a matter of days before they found you and brought you back."

"But you were the one who told the police?"

"I didn't tell the police. I swear to that. It was the detective I hired to find you, but those were not my instructions. He did it on his own."

"Sorry, but I fail to see the distinction you're trying to make."

"Excuse me, young woman. I couldn't help but overhear."

We both looked at Hunter, who was now standing beside me.

"I think you're mistreating someone who's a good friend. Josiah has taken care of your dog at her expense. She risked her life to retrieve your paintings, which had been stolen by a neighbor, and saved them for you. She got the best criminal lawyer in town to defend you. She came to visit you in jail. I don't see how you can have a better friend than Josiah Reynolds."

"She called the police on me when Toby accused me of trying to cut him with a knife."

"Again, she did the right thing. You were perhaps a danger to yourself and others."

"It was a lie."

"Maybe, but how was Josiah to know? She acted in accordance with the facts she had at the time."

Sandy pointed at me. "The first thing I thought when I heard she'd found Toby was she killed him."

I scoffed, "That's absurd."

Unfazed by the turn of the conversation, Hunter calmly pointed out. "Again, I remind you that you set fire to your own house, while burning Toby's possessions as well as his savings, and then staged a fake suicide–all with the intent to harm your husband. Of all people, you had the most to gain by killing your husband."

Sandy turned her attention back to me. "We're finished, Josiah. You stay away from me, you hear?"

Hunter and I watched Sandy storm off, presumably to the pathway that led to her burned house.

"I'm going to follow her," offered Hunter. "I want to make sure she leaves your property."

"I'm stunned. I don't know what to say except thank you for standing up for me."

"I didn't say anything that wasn't true. I'm going now, so go inside and lock the door. I shan't be long." He strode off to the left of the house.

Baby started to go with Hunter, but seeing me stay behind, whined, not knowing what to do.

"Come on, Baby. You hang with me." I scratched Baby's ears. "I know you're going to miss your friend Georgie. You were getting used to her, weren't you? She's with her mommy now. Let's be happy for her."

We went inside, locking the front door.

It had been an unnerving afternoon, going from my elation at Hunter's surprise visit to the trauma of Sandy's appearance.

I was flabbergasted at Sandy's attitude toward me.

I placed my Bible in my lap, but I didn't open it. I was too upset to read.

Maybe later.

But it turned out later would be too late.

37

"Ms. Todd, I'm recommending your client be evaluated immediately. Sandy Sloan may be delusional. She certainly wasn't rational when it came to Josiah. She could pose a significant risk to herself and others. Unhuh. Yeah," said Hunter, speaking with Shaneika on the phone in the great room of the Butterfly.

I was making tea, listening to the phone conversation on Hunter's end.

He continued, "I think getting her out on bail might not have been the correct thing to do. At least, we knew she was under supervision and being given her medication in jail."

Hunter motioned me to be quiet as I set the tea down on the coffee table.

I heard Shaneika on the other end, but couldn't make out what she was saying.

Hunter spoke again. "The problem is we don't know

if Sandy will behave violently or not. The story about her trying to stab her husband and eventually killing him may be correct. I find people who set fires are very disturbed, and Sandy's confrontation with Josiah was not rational."

I poured and handed a cup of tea to Hunter as he was listening to Shaneika.

He spoke again. "I followed Sandy to her house. Her car was parked there, and she left with her dog. However, I'm going to spend the night here. I don't think Josiah should be left on her own tonight."

My eyes widened at hearing that. I hadn't invited Hunter to spend the night, but thought it chivalrous of him to offer, knowing he loved to be at Wickliffe Manor. To tell you the truth, I wanted Hunter to stay, because I was a little shook up.

"Okay, but get back to me on this. Right." Hunter hung up.

"What did Shaneika say?" I asked.

"She agreed to the evaluation, and was surprised about the altercation. She said it was disheartening that her client would say those things."

"Where is Sandy staying?"

"Shaneika booked her a room at a modest motel in town." Hunter grinned. "I hope you don't think I'm being presumptuous, but I didn't like the intensity of Sandy's anger. She came very close to threatening you."

"I've never seen Sandy so angry. It was unnerving."

"Quite. I will stay here tonight, but I think you should make other arrangements until the trial is over."

"When is the trial?"

"Ms. Todd said in a couple of weeks, if she can't work something out."

"That's funny. Shaneika said I would be contacted by the DA's office, but I haven't heard a word from them."

"No subpoena?"

"No."

"She said she was working on a plea deal, so that may be the reason the DA hasn't contacted you. It would indicate the plea deal might be accepted."

Hunter poured milk into his tea. He must have picked up the habit when he lived in England.

I commented, "The only other person I know who pours milk in tea is Lady Elsmere."

"Speaking of Lady Elsmere, I think you should stay with her until this thing with Sandy blows over. I have to leave on another business trip soon."

"I don't know. I hate to intrude."

"Then how about having Franklin and his chap Matt, stay here?"

"Heaven's no. Matt has a baby. I couldn't impose. Out of the question. Speaking of Matt, have you met him?"

"Several times, but briefly. One time as I was coming to see you, Franklin and Matt were in the front yard of Matt's house playing with the baby. I stopped to say hello."

"I see."

"Matt is quite a stunner."

"Yes, he's very good-looking," I replied.

"He reminds me of some actor. Let's see, who was it? Oh, yes, the fellow who was in *The Robe*. Not Richard Burton, but the one with all the muscles."

"Victor Mature."

"That's the guy, but a more refined version."

"Victor Mature said he acted with his forehead."

"Did he?"

"If you watch him in the scene where he is standing at the foot of the cross when Jesus is dying, you will see he does."

"Interesting to know."

I remained silent.

"Are you still in love with him?"

"Who? Victor Mature?"

"Matt."

"What on earth are you yakking about?"

"Franklin says you're in love with Matt."

"Oh, Franklin says that about anyone who looks cross-eyed at Matt. If you want to know the truth, Matt is my dearest friend. We've known each other for a long time."

"I hear a but somewhere."

"Since he was shot, we haven't been as close. He has a baby now, and she takes up all his free time."

"You didn't answer the question."

"There was a question?"

"Are you in love with Matt?"

"It's none of your business."

"So that means yes."

"It means it's none of your business. I don't go prying into your past."

"Not yet."

Hunter and I glared at each other before breaking into laughter.

"Let's get back on track," Hunter said. "Will you make arrangements to stay at Lady Elsmere's?"

"I think it's a good idea. I'll also have her men watch my farm. I don't want any of my animals hurt. It's happened before."

I thought for a moment. "You know, it makes me angry I'm having to spend money on patrols for a person I tried to help." I thought back to what Kelly had said to me at Al's Bar.

"What are you thinking?"

"I was thinking about something a friend said to me recently."

"What?"

"He cautioned me to be careful about being used."

"I see. Sounds like good advice. Maybe you should take it."

"I don't like turning my back on friends. Where would I be without June, Matt, Charles, and Franklin? And Shaneika and her mother, Eunice, are like family. I couldn't live with myself if I didn't try to help my peeps."

"I hope you include me in that list."

Ignoring his comment, I said, "The question is—was Sandy Sloan ever my friend? I wonder. I certainly thought she was."

"Sandy is not a well woman. I wouldn't put much stock in what she's saying now. It might be her illness talking."

"I hope so. I've always been very fond of Sandy. I thought we were good friends. I'm heartbroken about the two of us having words, but I want to thank you for staying."

I was grateful. I really was.

After having our tea, I called Charles and told him what had occurred with Sandy. He promised to have his security team patrol my farm, and would step up security on Lady Elsmere's property as well.

We both have had episodes with deranged people setting fire to our property in the past. Remember Lacey Bridges, who torched Lady Elsmere's horse barn and killed Doreen DeWitt at Matt and Meriah's wedding, splattering the woman's brains all over my good suit? The last thing we needed was another Lacey Bridges on the loose.

What had Hunter said? People who set fires for emotional reasons are very disturbed.

Jumping Jehosaphat! What had I gotten myself into this time?

38

Hunter stayed the night and then the next. He installed several motion-activated cameras along the trail and put up No Trespassing signs.

As much as I disliked Darius, I told him Sandy was out of jail and making irrational accusations. "You'd better give up the rest of Sandy's paintings," I told him as he spat tobacco juice on the ground, some of it splattering on my canvas shoes. "She's a strong woman, and she's angry." I left it at that, hoping Darius would add two and two together—and come up with four.

Darius also put up No Trespassing signs to the chagrin of our neighbors on the right. The days of going through our property to the river were over—at least for now.

Hunter spent much of his time with his new horse, feeding her, brushing her, and finally riding her. He tried to get me to ride the Paint, but I wouldn't budge. I was afraid of falling.

I spent my time working, cleaning out a shed, and organizing my work tools. Exciting, huh! On the third day, Hunter announced he had to check on his house and go out of town on business.

I was grateful to Hunter. I really was, but I was starting to feel claustrophobic. I was not used to having anyone around 24/7 since Jake. (Walter Neff doesn't count.) I thought I had let go of Jake, but I was mistaken. I missed him. This realization made me want to go on a crying jag.

I needed to do some serious soul-searching, but one thing I knew was Jake and I were finished. Jake was the past.

Hunter might be the future. He was a nice man, with a good job. We had many interests in common. He knew which utensil to use at the table. He never wiped his nose with his sleeve. His wives lived on another continent. He had no children, which was a huge plus for me. You know how I feel about children. My standby retort about kids was the old W. C. Fields joke about how he liked children. He answered–parboiled.

So what was the problem?

39

Baby and I were spending nights at the Big House while Hunter was away.

In the mornings, Bess was kind enough to fix breakfast before I went back to the Butterfly. They didn't need me underfoot during the day.

And Lady Elsmere was kind enough to rise each morning before her usual time to join me.

"Would you quit feeding that mongrel from the table?" admonished June.

"Sorry, I didn't think you'd notice."

"I'm old, not blind." She pointed a diamond-laden claw at me. "Josiah, don't you dare wipe Baby's face with my napkins."

Bess yelled from the kitchen, "Is she using the good linen on that mutt?"

She stormed in with a roll of paper towels. "Here," Bess said, thrusting the paper towels at me. "You sure turn this house on its ear when you come."

"Aw, come on, Bess. You like dogs."

"Baby's not a dog. He's a horse who thinks he's a dog."

"Baby loves you, Bess. Baby, go give Bess some sugar."

Baby immediately rose and stood by Bess, leaning his head against her, wanting to be petted. In doing so, he smeared strawberry jam on her spotless white apron from the jam-loaded toast I had given him.

Exasperated, Bess let out a cry.

"What's all the commotion in here?" asked Charles, entering the breakfast room.

Bess complained, "Daddy, Josiah won't curb her critter."

A muscle in his jaw twitched, as Charles flashed his daughter a chastising look. "That's no way to treat a guest, and Baby is our guest. He's not a problem, if you know how to handle this breed of dog." He took the roll of paper towels from me and mopped Baby's face. "I wish you'd quit complaining about dogs in the house, Bess."

Charles clucked at Baby. "Come with me, Baby. I'll feed you." He moved toward the kitchen with Baby following, and Bess bringing up the rear, swatting at Baby's wagging tail.

I chuckled for I knew Bess was all bark and no bite. Bess would give Baby the best tidbits in the house to gobble down and brush his coat, which Baby loved. She just liked to complain. It was her thing.

I glanced at June, who was nibbling on a scone while reading the morning paper.

"Are you going to eat your bacon?" I asked.

"There's a whole tray of bacon on the table."

"I ate it."

June looked over her newspaper at the bacon tray. "I thought you wanted to become a vegetarian."

"I do, but when I'm nervous, I eat meat."

"Odd," murmured June, going back to reading the paper.

"Can I have your bacon?"

"NO! Quit being a pest."

I slumped back in my chair, shoving some toast in my pie hole.

"Are you pouting, Josiah?" asked June from behind her paper.

"No," I lied.

"Oh, dear."

"What is it? Something juicy I hope."

June put down the paper. "There's an article about Carol Elliott. She's officially missing." She handed the paper to me. "Read it, please."

Taking the paper, I looked for the article about Carol Elliott. Finding it, I read.

WINCHESTER WOMAN MISSING.
Venita Tuttle, mother of Carol Elliott, 38, went to the Winchester police on Thursday of last week to declare her daughter has been missing for almost two months. Mrs. Tuttle, when asked why it

took so long to go to the authorities, answered, "I was told she had left the town."

Mrs. Tuttle would not identify who had told her this.

The police searched the house of Carol and Lonny Elliott, 40, her husband, and also a plot of disturbed ground at the back of the property. Nothing was recovered which indicated foul play.

Venita Tuttle has issued a $5000 reward for information regarding her daughter's whereabouts.

Carol Elliott is 5'6", 146 lbs, with brown hair and brown eyes. Moon-shaped scar on left thumb. She was last seen wearing jeans and a long sleeved blue blouse with blue cloth buttons. Her hair was in a ponytail.

Venita Tuttle is asking for volunteers to help search the woods behind her daughter's home this Saturday starting at sunrise. The search will be coordinated by the Winchester police. Interested persons are to call 555-HELP. Donations will be gratefully accepted.

I folded the paper. "This case keeps getting muddier by the day. Toby's girlfriend has been missing for months."

June mused, "So Miss Carol couldn't have killed Toby."

"June, I have a favor to ask. I wouldn't be asking, but I don't have the money. Would you be willing to pay for Hazel Mott?"

"The woman with the Bloodhound?"

"She also has a German Shepard who's a trained cadaver dog."

"Josiah, I don't mind the money, but why do you care about Carol Elliott?"

"The sooner we find out who killed Toby Sloan, the sooner this whole mess will be cleared up, and Sandy can get on with her life."

"After the way she talked to you, I don't see why you give a damn. I get angry when I think of all the favors you did for her over the years. She pays you back with dumping her dog on you, and then rebuking you for taking care of it."

"Hazel Mott," I said, trying to get June back on track.

"You don't even know if the woman is dead, let alone missing. Carol Elliott could be sunning herself on a Florida beach with a new boyfriend."

"That story about a new lover is a red herring. Carol Elliott wouldn't have run off with another man if she had her heart set on Toby."

"You don't know that's true."

"You don't know that it isn't."

"If she is dead, she's probably buried in the plot of disturbed ground at the back of the house."

I frowned. "The police checked, and nothing was found."

"Oh, I remember now."

"Here's what I think, June. I think the dug-up ground was supposed to be a burial plot for Carol, but for some reason, it wasn't used. Probably due to the neighbor next door. She has a new baby, so she's up at all hours of the night. I think Carol Elliott is buried in the woods behind her house."

"You think the husband killed her."

"Start with those closest to the victim and work your way out."

"Given that supposition, Sandy is the logical person to have killed Toby."

"I'd hate to think it."

June thought for a moment. "Jo, I think we might be getting too old to play detective. Maybe we are delving into mysteries better left untouched by us."

"You feel this way because you're depressed about Liam being gone. You're giving up, June. Don't do that to me, old friend. I need you."

"You need my money."

"I need you."

June, genuinely touched, fussed with her napkin trying to hide her emotions. Regaining her composure, she asked, "If I give in to your request, will it get you and Mr. Slobber Puss out of my house sooner?"

"It might." I gave June my usual imploring look, which included thrusting out my lower lip and batting my eyelashes. Oh, the hoops I must jump through to get what I want, but it usually worked on the old girl.

June laughed. "Such a stupid face. It amuses me to no end to watch your feeble attempts at manipulation."

"Did it work?"

"Call your friend, Hazel Mott."

"Yippee! Thank you, June."

"I want you to do something for me, Jo."

"Yeah?"

"Be careful. You have a tendency to do too much for your friends. Many of them don't deserve your love. Just be careful. Will you–for me?"

The hair on the back of my neck stood at attention. This was a second warning from a friend.

What had they sensed which I hadn't?

40

A cop stopped us, instructing Charles to park in the church parking lot two blocks away.

Lady Elsmere lowered her window. "Young man. Has Helen Mott arrived with a cadaver dog?"

"A woman with a German Shepard came through here ten minutes ago. My sergeant told me to let her through."

"I paid for the dog's services, and I wish to personally witness if the dog discovers anything. As you can see, walking two blocks is out of the question for me."

The policeman tipped back his hat and scratched his head. "I don't know, ma'am."

"Please call whoever is in charge, and tell her Lady Elsmere wants access close to Carol Elliott's house."

The policeman reluctantly called in the request. He turned his back to us while talking. Finishing the call, the young man walked to the back of the Bentley, taking down the license plate number before waving us through.

Charles turned down Carol Elliott's street which was lined with parked cars. People, wearing boots and holding walking sticks, stood in little knots near her home.

Unable to find a parking space, Charles turned the car around and parked in the middle of the street. He got out and talked to a policeman who seemed to be guarding the Elliotts' house.

The policeman took Charles over to a plump woman standing in the driveway. The three of them talked for several minutes before the woman accompanied Charles back to the Bentley.

He opened the back door and stuck his head in. "Ma'am, this is Venita Tuttle, mother of Carol Elliott. She wishes to thank you."

Charles pulled back, and a woman with red-rimmed eyes, wearing a purple paisley headscarf and holding a handkerchief, bent over.

Lady Elsmere greeted, "Mrs. Tuttle."

"Lady Elsmere."

"Call me June, please. I'm just a Kentucky gal like yourself." She motioned to Mrs. Tuttle. "Please sit. You must be tired of standing and having folks stare at you. There's plenty of room." Lady Elsmere held her black-gloved hand out in welcome.

Venita Tuttle climbed in the Bentley while I scooted over to make room for her.

Settled, Mrs. Tuttle reached over and grasped Lady Elsmere's hand. "I want to thank you for providing the cadaver dog. I didn't have the money to pay for one."

Lady Elsmere reminded her, "You're offering a five-thousand-dollar reward."

Mrs. Tuttle dabbed her eyes with a soggy handkerchief. "I thought if anyone claimed the reward, I could sell my car."

"Ah, I see," replied Lady Elsmere softly. "I can tell you, I'm torn. I hope the dog helps, but if the dog should discover anything."

"I know," interjected Mrs. Tuttle. "Not knowing about Carol is terrible. You can't imagine. But if the dog finds something, that will be terrible too. Either way it's going to be a horrific day."

"Is anyone with you, Mrs. Tuttle?" I asked. "A friend or relative?"

"My husband is at home. He has a weak heart."

"So there is no one here with you?" asked Lady Elsmere.

Venita Tuttle shook her head.

Lady Elsmere shot me a compassionate look before stating, "Please stay with us in the car. I insist."

"I'm much obliged. I could wait in Carol's house, but Lonny's there." Mrs. Tuttle's voice hardened as she said Lonny's name.

"This is my friend, Josiah Reynolds. It was her idea to hire Hazel Mott."

"Hello," I said.

Mrs. Tuttle nodded before looking out the window. People were starting to gather outside the Elliott's house.

"Mrs. Tuttle, may I ask why the search hasn't started?" I inquired.

"The Captain thought it best to give the dog a head start. He's in the woods with Mrs. Mott right now."

"Why hadn't the police made any progress investigating Carol's disappearance before this?"

Lady Elsmere warned, "Josiah."

"I don't mind answering," said Mrs. Tuttle. "They believed Lonny's story about her running off with a man."

"Why are they here then?" I asked.

"After I made a public plea to have a search in the woods, they decided it would make them look bad if they didn't help."

"Surely not," objected Lady Elsmere.

"I'm sorry to say my Carol gave them reason to believe she had run away. I'm afraid her marriage was not a happy one. To a large extent it was her fault, due to her carousing behavior. Pour Carol's foolishness, other men, and an unhappy husband into a pot, stir constantly, and sooner or later there will be an explosion. I warned her, but she wouldn't listen.

"I don't mean to speak ill of my daughter. She's a sweet person, but when it comes to men, Carol doesn't have a lick of sense. I love her, though, and she loves me. She deserves better than this." Mrs. Tuttle drifted off talking, watching several policemen disperse the crowd.

I looked out my window to see people walking slowly to their cars on the street, casting glances at the Elliott's house.

Police began directing cars out of the cul-de-sac.

Lady Elsmere put her arm around Venita Tuttle.
"It may be nothing at all," she murmured to an anxious Venita Tuttle, who was watching people leave.

Mrs. Tuttle's eyes widened with fear. "What's happening? What's going on?"

"Stay here, Mrs. Tuttle. I'll see," offered Charles, who climbed out of the Bentley and headed over to several policemen huddled by the house.

I looked away. I couldn't witness Mrs. Tuttle's distress any longer. It was simply too painful to watch. I felt deeply for her, because I knew why the police were sending the volunteers away.

If Mrs. Tuttle didn't realize the significance of volunteers leaving, she made the connection when the coroner's van pulled into Carol's driveway. "Oh, God! Oh, God," she wailed, clawing at the door handle.

Lady Elsmere pulled her close. "I'm so sorry. So sorry, my dear. You must stay here. You don't want to see what they've found. You want to remember Carol as she was."

Wanting to give Mrs. Tuttle some privacy, I left the car and went into the backyard, thinking what an awful day this was for Venita Tuttle. Having closure was small consolation to a woman who had lost her child. I understood her pain, being a mother myself.

I clutched my chest as I waited for Hazel Mott to appear. I didn't have to wait long.

Hazel emerged from the thick woods with a huge German Shepard on a leash. Seeing me, she waved and strode over to me. "Howdy," she said.

"And?"

Hazel ordered her dog to sit before answering. He was panting heavily. "We found a skull with hair still attached. She had been placed in a grave, but animals must have smelled her and dug her up. She's scattered for miles, I bet."

"Can identification be made?"

"Naw. They'll have to do a DNA profile."

"What about her teeth?"

"Possibly. Possibly. Several of her teeth are missing. We couldn't find them. From the quick look I had of the skull, it looked like they had been pulled. I would also venture her hands will never be found either—cut off so no fingerprints. 'Tis a shame for sure. So young." Hazel slapped me on the back. "Well, gotta go. My dog needs to simmer down. Our job is done."

"See you later, Hazel. Thanks."

"Glad to help. Come on, boy," Hazel said to her dog.

I walked slowly to the Bentley.

We waited with Mrs. Tuttle until the Captain came over to talk to the grieving mother. He encouraged her to go home, explaining that the processing of the body would take hours, even days.

With his help, we arranged to take Mrs. Tuttle home while I followed with her car. We had a police escort for the ten-minute ride.

Venita's husband met her at the door with their pastor.

Relieved to know someone was with them in their time of grief, I gave the pastor the car keys.

He thanked me before closing the door.

I sadly went back to the Bentley.

We had to drive by Carol's street again to leave Winchester. A group of ghoulish onlookers had gathered at the entrance to the street, still blocked off with a barricade.

As we slowly passed, I saw Sandy Sloan standing in the crowd.

She turned and watched us pass.

It gave me the heebie-jeebies to see her there.

Immediately my mind began working.

Did Sandy Sloan have the strength to drag a 146-pound woman into the woods and bury her?

Perhaps the body was cut up first.

Could she have pulled out the woman's teeth?

Pulling out healthy teeth takes a lot of muscle.

I leaned forward and took another peek at Sandy before we were out of sight.

She was still watching at us, her hair blowing about her face.

"What is it?" asked June.

"Sandy Sloan is in the crowd."

June didn't say anything, but reached over and held my hand. Her fingers felt clammy.

I guess she was creeped out, too.

I couldn't wait for this day to end.

41

Believing the crisis was over with Sandy, I was sleeping at home again, and was having my breakfast when Shaneika stomped out on the back terrace. It had been a perfect morning until she showed up.

I looked up surprised. "Shaneika. What gives?"

She slammed her purse down on a lounge chair. "We're in big trouble, that's what."

"What do you mean?"

"Have you told anyone about sneaking into Carol Elliott's house?"

"Hunter."

"Why did you do that? It's another person to manage."

"Why are you so upset? Sit down. Have some orange juice." I handed a glass to Shaneika.

She plopped in a chair and drank it before speaking. "The police found Carol's diary. It confirms the story

Sandy told about Toby messing with her medication. Carol wrote Toby had told her he was substituting Sandy's medication with cornstarch. He wanted her to go off the deep end."

"So Sandy was telling the truth."

"Carol also wrote she was starting to feel afraid of Toby, and wanted to end the relationship, but he threatened her."

"If Carol wanted to end her affair with Toby, why would she call Sandy and brag about how she was going to marry him?" I asked.

"You know what I think?"

"Tell me, oh swami," I said.

"I think Toby killed Carol to keep her quiet."

"That's putting a different slant on things."

"Have you seen Sandy?"

"Not since she came to collect her dog."

"The police want to question her again, but we can't find her. She checked out of the motel."

"Wait a minute. I did see her. It was the day the police found Carol Elliott's body. She was standing in the crowd, gawking."

"That's another thing. The police interviewed the neighbors. The lady next door told them about a woman who went into the house, claiming she owed Carol money. They're looking for Sandy to see if she is the one, but the neighbor will undoubtedly say she is not the woman. The police will continue the search."

"Oops," I squeaked.

"Precisely. We're talking about a capital murder case here. If they find out I knew you were going to the house to snoop and you removed evidence, we both could go to jail. I certainly would lose my license. It would be considered tampering with evidence."

"I wore gloves and a wig."

"The witness said the woman walked with a slight limp."

"Ooops!"

"Precisely again."

"My lips are sealed if yours are. After all, you are my lawyer. Can't we claim 'privilege?'"

"As your lawyer, I can't advise you to destroy evidence, but as your friend, I'm telling you to burn the wig immediately. If the police find hair fibers, they can match it to the wig." She looked at her watch. "I'm due in court. If you see Sandy, call me"

"Why did you come all the way out here to tell me this? Why didn't you use the phone?"

"You must be kidding. You never know who's listening on the phone."

"And you say I'm paranoid."

"Burn the wig, Jo, before we're burned." Shaneika grabbed her purse and stormed out.

I exhaled and looked down at my breakfast now cold. It didn't matter. Shaneika's news had certainly put me off my food.

42

"Put your foot in the stirrup."

"I can't," I snapped. "My bad leg. It won't take my weight."

Hunter prompted, "Josiah, put your left foot in the stirrup. I will give you a boost and when I do, swing your right leg over the saddle."

"I'm afraid."

"You—afraid?"

"Yes."

"A woman, who has faced down some of the meanest hombres born on this earth, afraid of a little pony?"

"I'm not afraid of the horse. I'm afraid of hurting myself while riding the horse. What if I fall?"

"You're not going to fall. I've ridden her. She's very gentle," assured Hunter. "Ready or not." He pushed under my derriere, grunting ever so slightly. I had no place to go but up.

Abigail Keam

"Wait. Wait. Let me get my foot in the stirrup."
Hunter gasped, "Hurry up. You're heavy."
"In!"
"Now stand up in the stirrup and hold onto the horn.
Carefully swing your leg over in one fluid movement.
Try not to bang the horse with your right leg."
"You holding the horse?"
"I'm holding her steady."
The pony's eyes widened as she turned her head to
look at Hunter, a little unsure of what was taking place.
"Okay. Okay. I'm swinging my leg over. You know
I haven't done this in twenty-five years."
"MOVE IT! NOW SIT!"
I placed my fanny in the saddle, and slipped my right
foot in the stirrup.
The horse shifted which triggered protestations from
me. "Oh gosh! What's she doing?"
"You're around horses every day of your life, and you
don't know what she's doing?"
"Feeding horses apples across a fence is a whole lot
different from getting on their backs, and hoping they
won't throw you off."
"Big chicken."
"You got that right."
"I'm going to lead you, so you can get the feel of her
and let her get the feel of you."
"Right with ya, buddy," I whimpered.
"Open your eyes."

"Okay. Okay. I slowly opened my eyes and teetered back and forth slightly. Looking around, I prattled, "The ground looks so far away."

"Here we go," said Hunter, leading the horse around. "How does that feel?"

"I would have to say nice. Very nice indeed." I loosened my death grip on the horn, and leaned over, petting the horse's neck. "Good girl."

"What are you going to call her?"

"What was her name before?"

"Morning Glory. I think she was called Glory for short."

"Then Glory it shall stay. How ya doing, Glory? Nice day for a ride."

Hunter handed the Paint's reins to me. "I think you're comfortable enough. You do remember what to do with the reins?"

I snatched them from him. "Of course, I do. I'm not a total boob."

Hunter hoisted himself up on his huge Hanoverian and trotted over to me. His horse bumped into mine, which made my horse kick.

"Hey! Keep your horse away from my girl, Glory. I'm barely hanging on here," I protested.

"My girl is a little rambunctious. She'll calm down." Hunter assured.

"She'd better. No galloping now. Just walking."

"I'll lead the way." Hunter urged his horse forward, and Glory naturally followed. He kept the pace slow and easy. After I felt more comfortable, I urged Glory to the side of the Hanoverian, which was so tall I had to look up at Hunter.

"We must look a sight."

"Are you having fun?"

"Yes, I am, Hunter. Riding on a horse gives me a different perspective. What did Winston Churchill say about riding?"

Hunter quoted, "'There is something about the outside of a horse that is good for the inside of a man.'"

"That's it. It's like riding a bicycle, isn't it? You never really forget. I think I'm starting to get my confidence back."

"Do you think you could ride down a slope?"

"We better stay on level ground today. I don't want to take any chances."

"Next time then. We'll ease you into riding. Before you know it, you'll be galloping and jumping over fences."

"I don't think so, Hunter. There's no *National Velvet* here."

"Saw it as a child. About the Grand National, starring Elizabeth Taylor and Mickey Rooney in 1944. The horse's name was The Pie."

"I'm astonished. Are you trying to impress me?"

Hunter leaned over and tugged my hair. "Maybe just a bit."

I swatted his hand away, laughing. "Get on with you now."

We rode over to Lady Elsmere's property where she had several riding paths, and then near the foaling barn and back over to my stable. We stayed away from the pastures where the stallions were kept.

Mounting had been relatively easy compared to dismounting. I struggled to get the hang of it. In order to dismount, I would have to put weight on my left leg, stand, and shift my body so I could bring my right leg back over the saddle and step down.

Glory, sensing my discomfort, kept shifting her weight, which frightened me. Horses are very sensitive, and you must have confidence around them, which I did not. They become skittish if they think the rider is uneasy.

Frustrated, Hunter and my stable hand, Juan, found some old stairs English riders used to mount up. They sort of grabbed me with Hunter ordering me to swing my leg over and put my right foot on the stairs. The result was I was coming off the saddle head-down instead of feet-first, causing my left foot to get stuck in the stirrup.

Impatient, Hunter pulled my foot out of my boot, which dropped to the rubber floor and me along with it landing on my caboose. (Horse barn floors are covered with a rubber insulation floor to protect the horses).

"All you had to do was swing your right leg over," Hunter groused, picking straw out of my hair.

"Don't harangue me, Hunter. I don't like it when men are rough with me. I'm not gonna put up with it. I told you I hadn't been on a horse in years."

"You could dismounted on your own steam if you wouldn't worry about your left leg. You pamper it too much."

"Go jump in a lake."

Hunter sidled up to me and whispered, "Only if you go with me, Sugarlips. I haven't skinny-dipped in years."

"You're too much," I replied, chuckling. "Believe me, this is one body you don't want to see."

"There you go again. Putting yourself down."

"Oh, shut up, Hunter. Be happy I got on the darn horse. You have no idea how fearful I was about it."

"Franklin has told me how many times you have looked down the barrel of a gun and didn't flinch. How can you be scared of a little horse?"

"I didn't flinch because I tinkled in my pants. Tinkle isn't the right word. It was more of a flood."

Hunter nudged me playfully. "I'd pee in my pants too if someone pointed a gun at me."

"You're asking Franklin about me, huh?"

"He told me all about how you and this chap, Liam, and another guy captured a murderer who was killing women over jewels."

"Did he make me sound brave?"

"He made you sound awesome."

"Good."

"Were you and this chap Liam a thing?"

"Why do you ask?"

"Want to see who I'm up against. What kind of man

attracts a woman who takes down malicious thugs? Inquiring minds want to know."

"I never took down anyone. I had backup who did. Franklin likes to stretch a story."

Hunter nudged me again. "Well?"

"You're not up against anybody. Why do you care anyway? I couldn't care less about your past in that department."

"That's because I'm such a flop."

"And I'm not?"

"So you and this Liam weren't an item?"

"Goodness no. Liam was Lady Elsmere's boy toy."

"NO WAY?"

"Yes, way."

"Tell me more."

I started to relate the sad tale of June's infatuation with Giles, aka Liam Doyle of Ireland, when Tyrone pulled up in the Land Rover and honked. He motioned us over.

My limp was more pronounced now as I was walking with one riding boot on and the other off.

I must have looked comical. It was obvious Tyrone was smothering a grin by faking a cough.

"What's up?"

"Grandpa wants to see you ASAP."

"I'll have to change first. I smell like horse."

"He says now."

Hunter opened the car door. "Go on. It must be important."

"The horses."

"I'll take care of them. Now scoot."

I reluctantly hopped into the Land Rover, wondering what was so important that I needed to come immediately.

Tyrone sped off. The ride was bumpy requiring me to hang onto the door strap.

"I really should change," I murmured to no one. "Do I stink, Tyrone?"

"Ladies never stink. They might smell earthy, but they never stink."

"You should go into the diplomatic corps," I replied, teasingly poking Tyrone in the ribs.

"Hey, I'm driving. Behave."

"Tyrone, I rode a horse today. A horse!"

"Unhuh."

"Almost three years ago, I was lying on a cliff dying, but today I rode a horse."

"You sound like you're proud of yourself."

"I am. Very proud. What do you say to that?"

"I say we're here." Tyrone parked the car at the kitchen door of the Big House.

"Thank you, my good man." Tyrone and I bumped fists before I got out.

He pulled away.

I walked into the house wondering what was so important that Tyrone had to come for me. Perhaps it had to do with Liam. Maybe he was coming home.

Good news at last.

43

"Hello," I called out. "Anyone home?"

I heard a door open, and spied Charles walking down the massive hallway.

He motioned to me.

I bobbed over as fast as I could wearing only one boot.

Charles looked down at my feet. "Miss Josiah, you're carrying a boot."

"Tyrone said to come now, so I came."

"I did send him to fetch you. Mrs. Tuttle called Lady Elsmere, and her Ladyship was beside herself to tell you the news."

"So nothing bad has happened?"

"It depends on which side of the fence you sit."

"Lead the way then."

"She's in the library. I'll send in Amelia to help with your footwear. I don't do female apparel."

I made my way to the library hoping June didn't have another fire going. My hope was dashed when I opened the door. "June, it's roasting in here."

"Old bones, Jo. Old bones."

"And you're smoking those foul cigarettes as well!"

"Don't start nagging me again."

Leaving the hallway door open, I threw my boot in a chair before making my way to the French doors at the back of the room. "I'm going to let in some fresh air."

"I wish you wouldn't."

Amelia came in the room. "Where are you going to sit, Miss Jo?"

"I want her next to me," demanded June.

"I brought you some slippers, Miss Jo. Dad said you needed some help getting a boot off."

I sat down. "If you would be so kind. It's hard for me to take it off."

June asked, "How did the other boot come off?"

"Not by my own power, I assure you."

Amelia pulled off my boot and put the slippers on my feet.

"Thank you, Amelia. Can you please shut the gas off before you leave? We don't need a fire in the middle of summer."

"With pleasure. I'll have Bess bring some tea."

"No thanks," barked June. "We're going to drink bourbon. And close the door on your way out."

"Leave the door open. It's stifling in here," I said to Amelia, who was heading out of the room.

"Really," snorted June, watching Amelia leave the door open. "I need to remind Amelia who signs her paychecks." She leaned over and sniffed. "You reek."

"I've been riding, hence the boots."

"Really," she said again, but in an inquisitive tone.

"What did you want, June? Someone is waiting for me."

"Would it be the dashing Hunter Wickliffe?"

"June!!"

"Mrs. Tuttle called me an hour ago, and we had a long talk."

"What about?"

"Lonny Elliott has been arrested for the murder of Carol Elliott."

"So it was her husband."

"She said the police told her Lonny broke down and confessed during an interrogation. He told the police he found a note warning him that Carol was having an affair, and to check his wife's phone."

"Where did he find the note?"

"Someone placed it on his truck's windshield at work."

"Typed or written?"

"I didn't ask."

"Go on."

"Apparently, he checked Carol's phone, and listened to the messages. A lot of them were from Toby. You can imagine the type of message Toby might leave.

Lonny confronted Carol, and they had a huge blowup. She threatened to leave him, so he strangled her."

"Was the turned-up earth in his backyard to be a burial place for Carol?"

"It was just as you thought. The lady next door saw him digging up the patch in the middle of the night, so Lonny thought better of it."

"The police found droplets of Carol's blood in the basement, where he cut her body up."

"Did he pull out her teeth?"

"Yes, those with fillings. He even cut her hands off and threw them in the river, thinking that would prevent identification if the body was found."

"That's why Carol's wedding ring was in her jewelry box," I mused. "He must have cut her finger off."

June asked, "How do you know about her wedding ring?"

"Thinking out loud. Just a guess."

"It's a nasty business. No getting around it."

"How is Mrs. Tuttle doing?"

"Better than I would have expected. It was horrid for her to hear the details, but I think she was relieved. She said she was glad the police told her. She wanted to be prepared before the news hits the public. At least now there is some closure."

"I feel for her. It must be a terrible ordeal to lose a child in such a fashion."

"Did Lonny confess to Toby's murder?"

"The police asked, but Lonny swore he had nothing

to do with Toby's death. Didn't even know Toby was missing until he read about it in the papers."

That gave me pause. "Are you telling me this information in confidence?"

"Of course. I promised Mrs. Tuttle to keep the details to myself. She said I could tell you since it was your idea for the cadaver dog. Mrs. Tuttle asked me to tell you again how grateful she is."

"I think these are details Shaneika might need to know."

"You can't tell her. I'm sorry. I gave my word."

"If Lonny didn't kill Toby, who did?"

"Naturally he's lying. He killed Carol in a fit of passion. That's second-degree murder, but killing Toby is a capital case because it was premeditated. The death penalty could be on the table."

I agreed, "You're probably right, June. Lonny had motive and opportunity to kill them both. If you can stomach cutting up your wife's body, you can execute her boyfriend. Right?"

"Most assuredly."

But assured I was not.

I still had doubts.

44

Bookings at the Butterfly were nonexistent, and would not pick up until holiday weddings, which was fine with me. May and June were typically our busiest months, and Eunice made sure those months brought in a substantial profit. I had enough money to get me through until November.

When Eunice told me she was taking the rest of the month off, I silently rejoiced. I could have the Butterfly to myself. I relished having my privacy restored.

The trauma of early summer faded as life on the farm continued. Even reading in the paper Lonny Elliott had agreed to a plea deal for Carol Elliott's death didn't disturb my zen.

I had made my peace with the entire affair. I was content to let the business of arson and murder fade into the past. Even though I had lingering doubts about who was responsible for Toby's death, I didn't dwell on it. I had done all I could to help–some of my actions brought closure, and some of my good intentions were not successful. It was what it was.

I felt a little pang of guilt every time I talked to Shaneika Mary Todd. I had goaded her into taking Sandy's case, and now Sandy had disappeared, leaving Shaneika high and dry.

It would have been nice to let Sandy know the DA had dropped all charges against her. There was no direct evidence she started the fire at her house or was tied to the murders of Carol Elliott or Toby.

The DA's office interviewed me, and I truthfully told them even though Sandy had hinted at arson, she never actually confessed to starting the fire. Since the house was uninsured and insurance fraud was not involved, they decided to drop the entire matter.

That's great for Sandy, but what about Shaneika? Sandy hadn't paid her a dime, and now Shaneika was out what was owed her.

Shaneika groused, "Clients skipping town and not paying my legal fees happens more often than you think. I just put a lien on her property. Forget it, Josiah."

As the lazy summer drifted along, I did forget.

I rode Glory a couple more times, but Hunter was in the midst of serious renovation of Wickliffe Manor, so he didn't come over as much as he would have liked. Without Hunter, I didn't have the confidence to ride Glory, so I patiently waited, though Baby and I visited the Hanoverian and the Paint every day.

Walter Neff finally cashed my check after I went over to his apartment, and threatened to call the police for a wellness check if he didn't open his door. I think Walter was lonely and still not over the death of his lady friend, Bunny Witt, so he took it out on me. I let him scream and call me names, getting the poison out of his system. He stopped finally, from sheer exhaustion.

We took his beloved Avanti for a drive and had dinner at a seafood place along the river (of course, I picked up the check). We had a long talk.

Walter's mood brightened when I suggested Shaneika Mary Todd needed another investigator, and he should talk to her about it. Regardless of what I thought of Walter personally, he was a good shamus. When we parted, I hoped I had reached some sort of détente with him, but who knows with Walter?

Things seemed to be falling into place, and that's the devil's trap–complacency. Everything is fine and you let your guard down. You just don't see it coming.

I was getting ready for dinner at Matt's when I heard scratching at my front door. Thinking it was Ginger, Matt's dog, coming to play with Baby, I opened the door without checking my monitors.

"Georgie!" I exclaimed. "What in the world!" I quickly picked her up and looked around. No sign of Sandy, but she had to be nearby.

I quickly closed the door and locked it.

Georgie, not noticing my distress, kissed me with several licks and squirmed in my arms. When I let her down, she ran to find Baby. Seconds later, I heard yips of joy and heavy thudding, which I took to be them playfully chasing each other.

I remained stationed at my monitors, scouring the grounds for Sandy. "This is silly," I said to myself.

"Georgie. Georgie," I called.

She didn't come.

I found her nestled on my couch with one of Baby's chew toys. Baby was seated in front of her with a concerned look on his face, which Georgie ignored, happily gnawing away.

I called Shaneika's office. She wasn't there, so I left a message with her secretary that Sandy Sloan was back, and most likely at her house. Then I left a message on Shaneika's personal phone.

Gathering a leash, I clipped it to Georgie's collar. "Your mommy is probably looking for you. Let's take you home." I fed her a treat, and made sure she saw me put more goodies in my pocket. She leapt off the couch, jumped up on Baby one more time for good measure, and followed me without complaint.

It took all my strength to shove Baby back at the front door so he wouldn't come with us.

I hurried along the path near the top of the Palisades, hoping I wouldn't meet Darius Combs along the way. Since my golf cart was electric, it was silent, so Sandy couldn't hear me as I swung around the burned house, looking for her.

I saw Sandy before she saw me. It wasn't until I was in her peripheral vision she looked up, and then it was too late–for both of us.

I saw what I saw.

A shovel stuck in the ground next to a freshly-dug hole near the equipment shed. Beside the hole, I saw Sandy counting a wad of money from a tin can, which lay open beside her.

Another thing lay beside her. A shotgun.

But the thing that really caught my attention was a man's Omega Seamaster watch on her wrist. The stainless steel band caught the sun and shone, making it hard to miss.

The pieces of the puzzle fell into place.

"I brought your dog back, Sandy."

At the sight of Sandy, Georgie yipped and squirmed to be let down.

I tightened my grip on her.

"I was wondering where she had gotten to." Sandy slowly slid her hand along the ground until it rested on the shotgun.

"She wanted to play with Baby. Since you appear to be busy, I'll take her back to the house, and you can come for her when you're done," I suggested, playing for time.

Sandy picked up the shotgun. "I don't think so. Step out of the cart, please?"

"No."

"No?" Sandy grimaced. "You're such a tiresome person, Josiah. Get out of the cart and do what you are told, for once in your pathetic life."

"My friend, Hunter, is back at the house waiting for me," I lied, pressing on the cart's pedal to go.

Sandy raised the shotgun and blasted a tire at the rear of the cart.

I screamed, and Georgie frantically clawed me in fear, but I didn't let go. I could feel blood ooze from where she scratched me.

The adrenaline really kicked into my system. It was either flee or fight. I pressed the pedal again, which produced a grinding sound. The cart didn't move. It was too damaged. Fleeing was out of the question, so now I was going to have to fight.

I was mad. Real mad. If I was going to go down, I was taking this bitch with me. "I'm getting tired of folks pulling a gun on me and making threats."

"I guess you need to hang around a better class of people."

I held Georgie closer. I could feel her panicked little heart beating against my panicked big heart. "You wouldn't shoot Georgie, Sandy. You love her too much."

"Put her down."

"Not on my life. Georgie stays with me. If you make a move, I'll snap her neck."

"Looks like we have a Mexican standoff."

"I'm going to get out now, and when I get back to my place safe and sound, I'll let Georgie go." Not taking my eye off Sandy, I carefully scooted out of the cart, and slowly backed up with Georgie closely pressed to my chest.

Sandy took a step forward.

"Don't come any closer, Sandy. I'm trying to get out of here with nobody getting hurt. I get safely back to my house, Georgie runs back to you, and you leave. This event was a little misunderstanding between neighbors. Oh, by the way, all charges against you have been dropped. You're free to go wherever, and do whatever you want."

Sandy smirked. "That's the way I planned it. I knew the charges for arson were never going to stick."

"And Toby's murder?" I just couldn't keep my big mouth shut, could I?

"That, too. Have you figured it out?"

"Not until I saw your father's watch on your arm. There were only two places the watch could have been—down at the bottom of the river or with the murderer."

"I can tell you, since we're alone. I want to tell you. I want you to know. You always thought you were so smart. You bored me to tears with your pontification about art. Oh, the great Josiah with her PhD in art history. I would make fun of you to Toby after you left. He would laugh and laugh. We both thought you were a pompous ass."

I winced, because it hurt to hear Sandy utter those words. "I was a good friend to you."

"Yes, I guess you were, but I didn't care. I used you to make the connections I needed to sell my paintings.

"How could I have been so blind?"

"You were so blind to a great many things. You didn't even notice Brannon and me. We had a little thing going for a couple of months. You look shocked. You think Ellen Boudreaux was his only indiscretion?" Sandy laughed. "Oh, you poor sap."

"You're lying."

"No, dear, I'm not. Brannon was a notorious womanizer during the last years of your marriage. He made it with lots of your friends."

"Stop. Please stop."

"The truth hurts, doesn't it? The one thing I'm very good about is facing the truth."

"Like Toby cheating on you."

"I wasn't going to take it lying down, the way you did with Brannon. I spent years building my career, painting until my hands were raw from work, and sucking up to people like you. Then when I finally achieve a level of success, Toby decides he's tired of me, but not tired of the money I was bringing in.

"It was true about him messing with my medication. I knew what Toby doing, and I wasn't going to have it."

"So you killed him."

"And got rid of his little girlfriend, too."

"You placed the note on Lonny's car."

"I spent some time in Winchester asking around about him. Cost me a few bucks, but it was worth it. Found out Lonny had a filthy temper. I knew that gorilla would confront Carol. I was only hoping for a smackdown, but when he actually killed her–well, it was a bonus for me. Saved me the trouble of killing the cow myself."

"You were going to kill Carol and frame Lonny for it?"

"Like I said, he saved me a good deal of trouble."

'How did you find out about the affair?"

"She called and bragged about it. Remember, I told you."

"I know you're lying, Sandy. The police found Carol's journal. She wrote Toby had told her about messing with your medication, and she wanted to break it off. She was starting to get scared. Carol called to warn you about Toby, and you killed her for her kindness."

"Killing with kindness, that's me. Oh, don't look so upset, Jo. They both had it coming. You killed your own husband by aggravating him to death."

"Brannon having a heart attack due to stress in his life is hardly the same thing as blowing the side of your husband's face off with a shotgun, presumably with the one you're holding on me."

"I can say Lonny killed Toby."

"But you're the one wearing the Omega watch, the one your father gave Toby, which you took after you killed Toby. Then you released the brake on the truck letting it slide into the river. It threw me that Toby was killed near Winchester, making Lonny the natural suspect. Somehow, you must have made Toby think Carol was going to meet him."

"She had already been dead for weeks, but Toby didn't know that. He was going berserk not hearing from her, wondering what had happened. He just couldn't go to her house. He had to wait until Carol contacted him."

"How did you manage to make him think Carol had arranged a meeting by the river?"

"That's my little secret. You don't need to know everything."

I looked at the wad of money still lying on the ground. "That's Toby's share of the money. You burned enough money to make it look like you burned his half."

"Maybe. Maybe not." Sandy looked around. "I'll tell you something else about my husband. Toby bribed the surveyor to lie about our property line. The equipment shed is not on our property. Darius was right. That was my husband Toby, a weasel to the end. See why I had to kill him to protect myself? I knew what he had in store for me."

I remained silent, trying to figure out how I was going to get out of this mess.

"I'm so glad we've had this talk, Josiah, and cleared up a few things. Now give me my dog."

"I don't think so, Sandy." I took a step back.

"We both know you're not going to hurt Georgie. You don't have it in you."

I took another step back. "Yes, I will. I snap her little neck."

"Oh, Josiah. So predictable to the end. You don't have the nerve to hurt Georgie, but I do." Sandy raised her shotgun.

I dropped Georgie while turning to run, and stumbled on my own feet, falling flat on my face. I put my hands over my head and curled up into a ball.

There was the loud sound of a shotgun blasting away, causing me to tinkle on myself. I didn't feel anything, except for warm liquid between my legs. It took a moment to register, but there was no pain or blood oozing out of my body.

I heard movement, the rustling of grass, and Georgie's constant yipping.

"Get up, girlie. You ain't hurt except for your pride. Get up. I ain't gonna chew my cabbage twice."

"Darius?" I cautiously opened my eyes and peered from between my fingers.

Darius Combs stood a few feet from Sandy with his shotgun aimed squarely at her.

Sandy had dropped her gun and stood as if in shock.

"Git to my house and call the po-lice," Darius said, pronouncing police with a very long o.

"Am I shot?"

"The blast you heard was from my gun. I got the drop on Sandy. Now, git."

"Where did you come from? How did you know?" I was astounded I had been saved by Darius Combs, the meanest man on Tates Creek Road.

"Been keepin' an eye on this place. I knew she'd come back. That's why I took her paintings. I wanted a reason to jaw a spell with her.

"I've always been right suspicious Sandy kilt Toby. She was always full of malice. When she came back this morning, I'd hid and been watchin' her. You came along and got her to talkin'. I heard the whole, sorry thing."

Darius shifted his gaze to Sandy before spitting a wad of tobacco juice near her feet. "I told you, Josiah, her shed was on my propitty, but you never believed me, always taking Sandy's side of things."

"I was wrong, Darius. I'm sorry," I said, slowly trying to get up. Getting back on my feet was not as easy as falling on my feet.

Darius went over to Sandy and kicked the shotgun away.

"What did you shoot?" I asked.

"Your golf cart. The noise startled Sandy so much, she dropped her gun. Didn't see that comin', didja, girlie?"

I glanced at my cart. It was, indeed, shot all to hell.

Sandy fired back, "Shut up, Darius. It doesn't matter what you two say to the police. I'm disturbed. This encounter will only prove it. I was hallucinating when I killed my husband. The court will never send me to prison. I'll go to a nice mental facility and get out in two years. The notoriety will make the price on my paintings skyrocket."

As I made my way to call the authorities, I couldn't help but think Sandy was right. She would get out and have a good life, while Toby and Carol were rotting in their graves.

As for me, I had been a fool where Sandy was concerned. She never had any regard for me. I should have seen it. I should have been more discerning about my friend.

When will I learn?

Epilogue

Sandy's in jail waiting for the court system to sort things out. No bail this time, and she had to get another lawyer. Shaneika refused to represent her again.

One thing I did do before the police arrived was take five thousand dollars from the wad of money on the ground. I was determined to make sure Shaneika was paid one way or another. I also bought another used golf cart with Sandy's money.

Listen–there is justice, and then there is Kentucky justice–and Kentucky justice is raw and dark. Take it where you can find it. I make no excuses.

When I dropped the rubber-banded stack of cash on Shaneika's desk a week later, she didn't ask any questions, but put the money in a manila envelope and stashed it in her safe. She didn't even bother to say thank you. That's Shaneika for you.

Lo and behold, Darius took Georgie as a forever pet. I was hesitant about the arrangement, but they both seem to be happy. Georgie comes over frequently with Darius

in tow, for play dates with Baby. He sits in a chair
watching her play with a silly grin on his face. Everything
Georgie does is wonderful, according to Darius. Maybe
he's not such a jerk after all.

Glory and I are taking riding lessons. I'm keeping this
from Hunter. I want to surprise him with my new
riding skill. I don't know when that will be, since I
haven't seen him in a while. He's been busy or so he
says.

I don't put much stock in what people say anymore.
If Hunter wants to see me, he'll call. If he doesn't, he
won't. I'm not going to lose sleep over him, the way I
did with Brannon and Jake.

One thing I do know is that I have the love of my
daughter, Asa, and my dear friends, Franklin, Matt, and
Lady Elsmere.

And their love will do very nicely for now.

CPSIA information can be obtained
at www.ICGtesting.com
Printed in the USA
LVOW12s2035140517
534420LV00001B/4/P